Gunplay in the streets!

Longarm watched the man's eyes. Tiny beads of sweat stood out on his face. He looked like he was straining to lay an egg.

Then the man blinked and his right hand dropped to his revolver.

Longarm reached across his belt and drew his .44, ducking low and crabbing out into the street as he did so. The houseman's draw was fast enough, but he was sending the two rounds at the spot where Longarm had been, not where he was. As he swung around to correct his aim, Longarm fired up at the man's chest, hoping for a heart shot. Instead, he caught the man high on the left shoulder.

The houseman was still game. He went down on one knee and brought up his six-gun. This time Longarm took his time and planted a slug between his eyes.

*Also in the LONGARM series
from Jove*

TABOR EVANS

LONGARM

AND THE
RENEGADE SERGEANT

JOVE BOOKS, NEW YORK

LONGARM AND THE RENEGADE SERGEANT

A Jove Book / published by arrangement with
the author

PRINTING HISTORY
Jove edition / November 1988

ISBN: 0-515-09807-8

Jove books are published by The Berkley Publishing Group,
200 Madison Avenue, New York, New York 10016.
The name "JOVE" and the "J" logo
are trademarks belonging to Jove Publications, Inc.

Chapter 1

A sharp rapping on his door awakened Longarm. The woman draped over his chest stirred fitfully and rolled off him and over onto her back. In a second she was snoring again. The rapping on Longarm's door came again.

Longarm flung his bedclothes aside and sat up on the edge of his bed, fighting off the tentacles of sleep that still clung to him. He was exhausted. This woman beside him had kept him awake most of the night with some of the most delightful variations on the act of love he had ever encountered in a long and glorious career. The thing was, all that gymnastics had drained him so, he had overslept.

The rap came again, more urgently this time. He glanced balefully at the door. "Who is it?" he demanded sharply.

1

"It's me, Longarm," came the breathless voice of Henry, Marshal Billy Vail's clerk. "The marshal told me to come get you. He said you got to catch a train at one o'clock!"

The woman beside Longarm stirred sluggishly and sat up, the bed sheets dropping away from her magnificent breasts. She ran a hand through her long, black, glossy hair and blinked sleepily at him, obviously disturbed by all this rapping and yelling through Longarm's door.

"Tell Billy I'll be in before twelve," Longarm told Henry irritably through the door.

"It's twelve now!"

Longarm thought fast. "Then tell Billy to meet me at the train depot with my tickets."

"You sure, Longarm?"

"You heard me. Now, scat!"

Longarm heard Henry turn from the door, race down the hallway, then plunge down the stairs.

Scratching his head, he leered at Dolores DeSalle. "That gives us plenty of time," he assured her, one hand closing gently about the marvelous silken globe hanging closest to him.

As he pulled the rest of her under him, he heard her contented sigh as she locked both arms about his neck and opened her mouth for his kiss. . . .

As Dolores, her back against the headboard, combed out her waist-length hair, Longarm, naked as a jaybird, padded over to his dresser. Through the open window came the odor of burning leaves and the equally unmistakable odor of horse manure and coal smoke. Somewhere a dog barked. Glancing into the mirror, he

2

glimpsed Dolores, bare-chested and lovely as a siren, combing out her hair in long languorous strokes. He sighed. This one, he would miss.

Then he concentrated on his own image. It was a lived-in face he saw staring back at him. An unblinking sun and unforgiving winds had cured his rawboned features to a saddle-leather brown. He might have been mistaken for an Indian if it had not been for the gun-metal blue of his wide-set eyes, the tobacco-leaf color of his hair and longhorn mustache, and the dark stubble on his lantern jaw.

A train entered the Union yards a quarter mile away and let loose with a long, quavering whistle, reminding Longarm that he had better haul ass if he was not to get rained on by Billy Vail. Reaching for the bottle of Maryland rye on the dresser, Longarm took a healthy belt to settle himself down some, then set to work making himself presentable.

He shaved using the last of the rye and the water from the pitcher on his commode, then turned and asked Dolores to hand him his long johns.

She chuckled lowly, her eyes glinting mischievously. "Do I have to?" she asked. "I like you just the way you are."

"Indecent female," he told her. "Have you no shame? I thought your eyes were averted all this while."

She handed him the underwear. "I think you were showing off."

"And if I was?" he asked, grinning.

"I must admit. I enjoyed every minute of it."

Chuckling, Longarm stepped into his long johns, and plucking his gray flannel shirt from where it hung on a bedpost, he quickly buttoned it up and reached for the brown tweed trousers hanging on the other bedpost. He pulled the britches on and cursed the fly shut. The pants fit like a second skin around his thighs and hips, a practical necessity for a man whose travels occasionally took him into brushy country, and whose job was such that a pair of pants caught on a bramble at the wrong moment might make a mortal difference.

He sighed slightly as he took a black string tie from the dresser and knotted it under his shirt collar. Some bureaucrat back in Washington had decided that federal employees had to wear these damned nooses around their necks while on duty, though Longarm usually shed the fool thing once he was out of sight of the home office.

Bending double, he pulled on a pair of woolen socks, then grunted his feet into his cordovan cavalry stovepipes. They were low-heeled and as tight as his pants because, as a working lawman, he spent as much time afoot as he did astride a horse, and could run with surprising speed for a man his size in boots that fit as tightly as these did—a fact that many an unhorsed outlaw had learned to his dismay as he hobbled frantically over the landscape in high-heeled boots with Longarm in pursuit.

Longarm slipped the supple leather belt of his crossdraw rig around his waist, adjusting it to ride just above his hipbones, checked the load of his double-action .44, and dropped it into the holster. Then he put on his vest, after which he swept the change off the top of his dresser and dropped the money into his pants pocket. Then he picked up his wallet. He had only a single twenty-dollar silver certificate in it—not nearly enough to last him until next payday, unless he got lucky at poker somewhere. His silver federal badge was pinned

4

inside the wallet. He rubbed it once on his shirtsleeve, then folded the wallet, put on his dark-brown frock coat, and slipped the wallet into his inside pocket.

A handful of extra cartridges and a bundle of waterproof kitchen matches were in the right pocket of his coat. The left one held his pair of handcuffs. The keys to the cuffs and his room he slipped in beside a jackknife resting in his left pants pocket.

Then, with some care, Longarm lifted the Ingersoll watch from the top of his dresser. Attached to the watch was a long, gold-washed chain. Clipped to the other end of the chain was the brass butt of a double-barreled .44 derringer. The watch rode in the vest's left breast pocket, the derringer in the matching pocket on the right, the chain looping across Longarm's nearly flat vest-front between them.

Ready now for the world, Longarm tucked a clean linen handkerchief into the breast pocket of his frock coat, then lifted his snuff-brown Stetson from its peg on the wall and positioned it dead center on his head— tilted slightly forward, cavalry style. Picking up his already packed carpetbag with one hand, his Winchester with the other, he turned to look directly at Dolores.

She was still combing out her hair and reminded him of a mermaid preening herself to lure foolish seamen onto her treacherous rocks.

"Time to bid you good-bye," he told her reluctantly.

She put down her brush and arranged two long shimmering waves of coal-black hair so that they framed her luminous breasts. Thrusting them out provocatively, she asked, "Are you really leaving me now?"

"Of course. You heard Henry. I have to meet Vail at the train depot."

"Then you're leaving Denver?"

"That's what it looks like. Billy Vail made some mention of it yesterday. But he didn't give me any details."

"How long will you be gone?"

"He didn't say. He couldn't. It all depends on my assignment."

She tipped her head slightly as she regarded him. "Then you really *are* a federal marshal."

"That's what I told you last night."

"I never believe what men tell me."

Longarm grinned. "That's a wise policy."

"Could I remain here—until you get back?"

"I thought you were staying at the Windsor."

"But you know how expensive the Windsor Hotel is, Custis."

He thought she was going to pout. To forestall it, he nodded quickly and started for the door.

"Aren't you going to kiss me good-bye?"

He paused at the door and smiled back at her. "I don't dare chance it," he told her, shifting the Winchester to his left hand and pulling open the door.

As he moved down the stairs, his knees were weak. And he found himself hoping that whatever assignment Marshal Billy Vail had for him did not take too long. He was already anxious to get back to that woman he had just left in his bed.

Longarm met Marshal Vail in the middle of the station platform. As the older man turned at Longarm's approach, Longarm caught the relief in his face.

"I'm real pleased you could make it," Billy Vail told him with his usual, heavy-handed sarcasm. "Your train pulls out in fifteen minutes."

"You didn't tell me much yesterday, Billy. What's this all about?"

"You said you wanted to get out of Denver for a while, so I'm just trying to be obliging."

"I changed my mind. I met someone very warm and interesting last night."

"Too late for that."

There was a restaurant in the depot. Vail led the way into it and found a table near a window facing the platform. Longarm placed his carpetbag down beside the table and leaned the Winchester against the wall. A waitress hurried over and both men ordered coffee.

Marshal Vail took off his derby and placed it down on the seat of an empty chair, then leaned forward and screwed his full face into a frown as he considered how to begin. In his salad days, Billy Vail had ridden many an outlaw's ass into the ground, but he had long since gone to lard. His sagging jowls and protuberant belly served as an ominous warning to Longarm of what could happen to him if he didn't stay in the saddle and on the move.

"This thing is very sensitive," Vail began. "It needs what the boys in Washington call discretion. And since you did so well tracking that hired killer for us a little while ago, you've been elected to handle this one."

"I'm flattered. Will I be gettin' another bonus?"

"Not this time. It's the army that's behind this, and you know how cheap the War Department is."

Longarm smiled wearily. He knew. Their coffee arrived. Longarm pulled his cup toward him and sipped the brew. His whole life flashed before him and he wondered if there was a regulation somewhere that ensured railroad coffee would always taste this bad.

7

"Let's have it, Billy," Longarm said. "That one o'clock train'll be here soon and this coffee is liable to kill me."

"About six years ago in Arizona, on the way back to Fort Apache from Fort Leavenworth, an army paymaster and his detail were ambushed and wiped out."

"I thought army paymasters always had escorts."

"Usually, yes. And after this debacle, always. But this time it had none because of some trouble with a local band of Apaches and some toughs in the mining camps close by. But a lieutenant Brent, a Sergeant Cable, and ten experienced troopers headed the detail. Remember the name of that sergeant. Cable."

"First name?"

"Paul."

"Why should I remember Paul Cable?"

"I said the detail was wiped out. It was. Except for this one single son of a bitch."

"He escaped?"

"Better than that. He planned the whole thing."

"How do we know that?"

"There was a freighter on the trail ahead, hidden by the rocks and terrain. He heard the shots, pulled his wagons to a halt and took cover in the rocks and waited. When the shooting died down, he circled back on foot and found one trooper alive, the pay chest blown, and the twenty thousand in gold gone. Before he died the trooper said it was Sergeant Cable who had shot him."

"Twenty thousand in gold, you say?"

"Yes. That *is* a lot, and it was quite a haul. The men at the fort had missed quite a few paydays, it seems, and they were getting damned restless. This was one of the reasons why the detail was sent without a proper escort."

8

"Six years ago this was?"

"Yes."

"Isn't it a little late for the army to be looking for the sergeant?"

"The army has never stopped looking for this man, Custis. And it never will. The trouble was, they didn't know where to look."

"But now they do?"

Leaning forward, Vail took a letter out of his inside breast pocket. "Two months ago the War Department got this letter from a retired officer. He says he ran into Sergeant Cable near a small mining camp close to the Arizona border. Cable is a prosperous rancher and owns a good part of the town and has surrounded himself with a small army of gunslicks."

"And the army wants him back."

"In leg irons, preferably."

"Why doesn't the closest army post send out a detail and bring him in?"

"It's all in this letter. Sergeant Cable is going by the name of Jim Gettis. His ranch is close to the border. If any military shows up, Gettis simply drifts into Mexico and stays there till the army clears out."

"And you want me to go down there and haul him in."

"You know the country well enough. You've been in that neck of the woods before."

"Yes, I have, chief. As you once described it to me, it's impossible country—the other side of the moon with a sun that would make an omelet out of your spit in seconds. Razor-sharp peaks, eroded wastelands, twisting canyons without an end—a playground for scorpions, sidewinders, and Gila monsters." Longarm

9

grinned. "Yeah, chief. I remember all right. What's the name of this mining town?"

"Copper City."

"How do I get there?"

"Train. Then stage. Your tickets are in this envelope along with that retired officer's letter. You can get what else you need at Fort Apache."

"Sounds like another undercover job."

"Well, it sure as hell won't do you much good to ride in blowing a trumpet. Just use your discretion on this one. Handle it any way you want, but bring that bastard in."

"Dead or alive?"

"That's up to you, Custis. But as a matter of fact, the army would very much like to put this deserter on trial, make an example of him—then hang him high."

"Isn't there a good chance he could beat the rap? After all this time, where you going to find witnesses? Besides, he's a civilian now, with a new identity—and maybe some pull with the territorial governor."

"If you bring him in, he'll be tried for complicity in murder. If the army can't make that stick, he'll be tried for grand larceny, and if that doesn't wash, he'll be tried as a deserter."

Longarm nodded, satisfied.

At that moment the restaurant began to tremble slightly. Longarm finished his coffee, then glanced out the window to see the passengers moving out toward the edge of the platform, every one of them peering down the tracks at the approaching train. Its distant tolling as it approached the depot sounded clearly through the restaurant's walls.

Longarm stood up. "Here's my train," he said.

10

"Good luck, Longarm," Billy Vail said, handing Longarm the envelope.

Longarm took the envelope from the marshal, then lifting his carpetbag off the floor, he grabbed the Winchester and headed out of the restaurant, leaving Vail to pay for the coffee, the first time in a long time Longarm had been able to stick his chief with the tab.

Chapter 2

Longarm stepped down out of the stage into the blazing Arizona sun and waited for the stage driver to hand him down his carpetbag and Winchester. The stage driver flung the carpetbag down carelessly and it kicked up dust at Longarm's feet. He was more careful with the Winchester when he saw the look in Longarm's eyes and handed the weapon to him.

Leaving the express office behind him, Longarm went in search of a hotel. He was not happy with the selection that offered itself to him as he trudged along Copper City's main street. He passed two one-story frame structures that offered a wooden bunk, a pillow filled with hay, and maybe a sheet, for two bits a night. There were some accommodations that were even cheaper and dirtier. Longarm had no difficulty imagining their seldom-washed blankets, broken mirrors, brown soap in sardine cans, and water barrels crawling with wiggle-tails.

He kept going and came at last to the Copper City Palace Hotel, a ramshackle three-story affair that proclaimed itself "The Finest Hotel South of Denver," a boast that did not even draw a chuckle from Longarm as he mounted the narrow porch steps and shouldered his way into the lobby.

It was a shabby, stifling place, graced by a single threadbare rug. In places, rough miners' boots had already worn holes in it. A few potted palms carelessly placed about had long since wilted and given up the ghost. The cuspidors were caked brown with dried tobacco juice, the carpet around them stained a rich mahogany.

The desk clerk seemed dazed by the heat. Longarm asked him for a room and took what the fellow offered without argument, mounted the narrow stairs to his room, found his key useless in the broken lock and kicked the door open. He dropped his bag onto the bed and leaned his Winchester against the wall by the headboard. The bed was a corroded-green brass affair that sagged in the middle. A water pitcher and an enameled bowl sat on a mail-order dresser beside the window. A fine patina of dust covered everything. The shade over the window was hanging crookedly, and when Longarm stepped over and attempted to adjust it, the entire assemblage came crashing down, raising a thick cloud of dust in the process. Since there was no way Longarm could repair the shade, he gathered up its fragments and dumped them in the corner, wooden roller and all. The sun now blasted through the window in a single, powerful beam that lit up every single dust mote.

Ignoring its intrusive presence, Longarm pulled off

his boots, placed his hat beside him on the coverlet, and lay back on the bed. Its lifeless sag did not entirely dismay him, grateful as he was for the fact that it at least remained still under him—unlike that interminable, swaying, creaking ride on the stage. He had kept himself braced in a corner of the infernal contraption, but it had not helped all that much. He removed his Colt from his holster and placed it under his pillow. With his fingers closed about its grips, he dozed fitfully until the sun dropped behind the mountains, after which he passed into a quick dreamless sleep.

When he awoke an hour or so later, he pulled on his boots, clapped his hat back on, and went in search of nourishment. He found it in a crowded restaurant called Stella's Eats. Stella was blonde and large, with a crew of Mexicans under her tyrannical gaze. Despite her bulk, she piloted her course through the crush of tables as lightly as a gas-filled balloon. Despite the heat and the dark patches of perspiration that ran down from under her enormous arms, she remained determinedly cheerful to the patrons she served. His stomach filled adequately with a generous portion of beefsteak, fried potatoes, grits, and several large mugs of black coffee, Longarm left Stella's and took a walk to the end of town to get some idea of its layout.

Copper City, as he had noticed earlier in the approaching stagecoach, was nestled in the foothills of a spiky mountain range, the distant peaks of which were now changing from bright rust to blue as the sun's light rapidly faded. The range would soon be purple, he realized, and the cool desert night would be upon them.

Returning, Longarm took a back route, coming in through the southern portion of the town. He found himself walking down narrow back alleys and filthy, rutted lanes crowded with tents and crude shanties. The stench of the privies was heavy on the wind. It was in this squalid section where the cribs of the town's prostitutes were located. Passing their tents, he glanced in at the Cyprians waiting for the night's business, shuddering at the mean, pathetic looks of the young, mostly Mexican, girls. Some stirred hopefully from their cots at his approach, but he kept on, glad to leave them behind and return to the more prosperous, less gamey section of town.

Despite the lateness of the hour, Main Street was a tangle of freight and ore wagons on their way to and from the mines and the mills. Copper City apparently paid no heed to the clock. Everyone and everything remained on the move. A perpetual cloud of dust hung over the street and the one- and two-story adobe buildings. As he kept on, dusk settled over the town and lamps began to glow in some of the stores. He noted that while many of those crowding past him on the packed-earth sidewalk were Mexican, a majority of them appeared to be Welsh, judging from their ruddy complexions, their blue eyes—and their swaggers. They had reason to swagger. Men from Wales were the best miners in the world.

And the toughest.

By this time Longarm was ready for a drink and crossed the street to the Long Chance Saloon, a big, high, one-story adobe building set off by itself with alleys on both sides. Kerosene flares on either side of the big open doorway lighted the entrance. As Longarm pushed his way into the saloon, the sound that washed over him was like a physical blow.

The room was vast. A bar ran its length. No bottles were in sight, and no mirror backed the bar—a wise

16

precaution for the owner, since it meant he did not have to replace it after every brawl. A half-dozen shirtsleeved barkeeps were serving the men who jammed the bar's entire length, and along the other side of the room facing the bar, Longarm saw four large round poker tables, every chair occupied. There were four faro layouts against the rear wall, and perched on a high stool in the corner was a single guard watching the poker tables and the faro operation closely, a shotgun resting across his lap. The high ceiling, from which a dozen lamps hung, was almost invisible because of the thick, swirling clouds of tobacco smoke that filled the room.

Longarm edged his way through the crush to the bar. When he managed to catch the attention of one of the barkeeps, he ordered a beer. After paying for it, he moved, beer stein in hand, through the crowd toward the faro layout. It was getting quite a play, the crowd around it two- or three-men deep, and he wondered why.

As he pushed through the crowd, a burly houseman armed with a sawed-off pool cue pushed Longarm arrogantly aside as he swept past him. Longarm heard the commotion coming from behind him then. He paused and looked back. A wild fight had exploded in the front of the saloon. As Longarm watched, two burly bouncers joined the one that had just pushed past him and plowed through the crowd toward the commotion. In a moment, pool cues flailing, the three bouncers quelled the disturbance and dragged the now unconscious troublemakers from the saloon.

Turning his attention back to the faro table, Longarm kept on through the crowd surrounding it and discovered at once why faro was so popular in this saloon. It was the nature and gender of the faro dealer. The dealer was female—every inch of her—a blonde, handsome, striking woman in her early thirties, wearing a green, long-sleeved blouse. She was ripe but not overripe, full but not bulging. A seasoned dish for a gourmet, Longarm realized. Like most professional gamblers, she had an utterly expressionless face and was careful never to look at the players who were betting. Win or lose, she showed no emotion as the case tender, in a husky, indifferent voice, called the cards as they came out of the case.

"Who's the blonde?" Longarm asked a miner beside him.

"That's Casey," the man said, a hushed awe in his voice.

Casey was something, all right, and it was obvious she did not lack for champions in this place. Evidence of the respect these unwashed miners held for her was the surprising decorum and lack of swearing about the gaming table. Even losing players kept their mouths shut and took their losses in stride. It looked to Longarm, in fact, that the game did not matter as much as the opportunity it gave them to be near Casey.

Longarm moved closer to get a better look at the play. A sharp, rasping voice cut through the din.

"You there! Bet or move off!"

Startled, Longarm looked quickly about him—then saw the eyes of everyone staring at him and realized it was the guard with the shotgun who had spoken and that he was addressing Longarm. Longarm turned his gaze full on the man. His eyes had the consistency of weak soup and his tobacco-stained mustache barely hid a mean, thin-lipped mouth.

Longarm did not see any reason to get riled at the man's tone. It was obvious he didn't know any better.

He raised his beer stein in salute to acknowledge the guard's presence, and remained precisely where he was and continued to watch the blonde faro dealer. From where he stood, he was not disturbing the play any, and as he saw it, as a patron of the place, he had as much right to stand where he was as did anyone else.

A piercing whistle cut through the noise of the place. Before Longarm could figure out what it meant, he felt a rough hand grab his arm. He turned and saw one of the bouncers, his sawed-off pool cue in his hand. He was raising it behind his head, threatening to use it on Longarm.

"All right, mister," the bouncer growled. "Outside— and pronto."

Longarm yanked his arm out of the man's grasp. "Or you'll do what?"

The men closest to them pushed hurriedly back, aware that quick and bloody trouble was on the way. Out of the corner of his eye, Longarm saw the guard with the shotgun jump out of his chair and bring up his weapon.

"If you want a demonstration of how I use this pool cue, mister," the bouncer said, "just let me know."

Longarm had not suffered gladly during that long, interminable ride in the stagecoach through alkali dust and glare over the hottest stretch of flatland he had ever traveled. It had been like walking barefoot over a hot stove and not being able to jump off. Now the bottled frustration of that ride burst from him. Hardly thinking, he grabbed the bouncer's shirt collar and flung him about, planting him between himself and the guard with the shotgun.

Then he flung what beer was left in his stein into the bouncer's face, momentarily blinding him. Enraged, the houseman swung wildly at Longarm's head. As the cue whooshed past inches from his skull, Longarm, still holding the man by the shirt collar, slammed his beer stein into the man's face. The blow crunched his cheekbone and smashed his nose flat without breaking the glass. Then, still using the stein as a club, he caught the bouncer on the side of the head, clubbing him until he dropped to his knees. Another shrill whistle came from Longarm's right, but he paid it no heed as he snatched the bouncer's pool cue from his grasp and brought it down on top of the man's head. As the bouncer plunged forward onto the floor, his bloodied snout plowing up the sawdust and mud covering the floor, Longarm decided it was time for him to take leave of the place.

Another shrill whistle filled the awed, near-silent saloon. Longarm dove into the crowd and bulled his way toward a door he had sighted at the back of the room. He glanced back at the guard with the shotgun and saw the man advancing around in a fury, trying to get a clear shot at him, one that would not hit any of the paying customers.

Ducking through the open doorway, Longarm headed down a dimly lit corridor, heading for the black rectangle of the open back door. As he reached it, he heard the pounding of heavy, booted feet as the other bouncers came after him. He broke out into a dark alley and dodged left as a gunshot roared behind him. It slammed harmlessly into a wall farther down. A stack of beer barrels loomed out of the darkness ahead of him. With a sudden smile, he skirted them, then turned about and sent them rumbling back toward his pursuers. Resuming his flight down the alley, he heard the barrels crashing to the alley floor and rolling on into the night. He heard one of his pursuers cry out as a barrel slammed him in the shins. Another cursed as he was bowled out of the way.

Longarm looked back. A small army of men was pouring out of the rear of the saloon. Turning back around, he increased his speed and kept going until he saw ahead of him two men coming to a halt at the mouth of the alley where it emptied onto a side street.

They were craning their necks, listening.

At once Longarm held up so they would not hear his running footsteps. He looked quickly behind him. A few of those chasing him were carrying lanterns now, their bobbing lights sending grotesque shadows dancing ahead of them as they ran. If those two waiting at the head of the alley remained where they were, Longarm was trapped. Moving close to the rear of a two-story frame building, he moved along it to the alley mouth, passing what appeared to be an open, curtained window on a level with the alley. Only a few feet beyond it, he saw the two men duck swiftly into the alley and head toward him. They must have caught Longarm's movements in the darkness.

Ducking quickly back to the open window, Longarm extended his arm, brushed aside the heavy curtains and stepped into the room, careful to draw the heavy curtains shut behind him. Inside the room the darkness was absolute. He kept perfectly still and listened to the muted shouts of the men racing down the alley toward him. Then came the pounding steps of the two men who had hurried into the alley to cut him off.

A woman's voice came from directly behind him. "I have gun. I am not afraid to use it. I think maybe you better leave same way you came in."

The voice did not quaver and had a strong, husky quality to it that Longarm liked. In the darkness he smiled. "I won't hurt you, ma'am," he replied softly. "But I would rather not go back out there. It's me they're after."

"I am not so dumb I do not know that. Why are they after you?"

"One of the bouncers at the Long Chance tried to flatten my skull with his pool cue."

"Ah! And you do not let heem do this thing?"

"This is the only head I got."

She chuckled softly. "Stay where you are."

The faint creaking of bedsprings came from a bed behind him, then a rustle of cloth, followed by a rasping of a match—and Longarm saw a tall, slim ebony-haired Mexican woman, no more than twenty-five, light a lamp's wick, then replace the chimney. She turned up the wick, picked up a revolver from the night table beside her and stepped to one side, holding the lamp up beside Longarm to get a better look at him. The two regarded each other in silence. Longarm liked what he saw very much, and he hoped the woman might be equally impressed.

She had already retired for the night, apparently, and was wearing a blue nightgown that did not quite reach the floor. He could see the toes of her bare feet curled up slightly to keep them off the chill of the earthen floor. She had braided her long black hair, the two gleaming braids hanging forward over her shoulders, past trusting breasts that amply filled out the front of her nightdress. Her neck was long and graceful and her face had clean, aristocratic lines, with high cheekbones, eyebrows that canted slightly, and large, coal-dark eyes that glowed like jewels in their sockets. Her mouth was firm and full, her chin square, a tiny cleft in it.

Of all the windows in Copper City he could have

climbed into, he had certainly chosen the right one this time.

Muffled shouts came from the alley. The girl turned her head to look at a door leading from this bedroom into the alley. Waving her gun at him, she said, "Get over in that corner, away from the window."

Longarm moved past her dresser into a curtained-off corner that served as her closet. The woman put her gun on the table, picked up the lamp, and moved over to the door. Unlocking it, she flung it open and stepped out into the alley. The confused and high-pitched jabber of the men milling about in the alley just outside her window died abruptly.

"What is all this noise out here?" the woman demanded.

There was a nervous pause—then a man spoke up, almost apologetically: "We're lookin' for someone, Miss Carlotta."

"Do you have to wake up the dead to do thees?"

Another male voice, revealing considerably more command, spoke up, "You seen him, Carlotta? He must have passed close by your window there."

"If he did, he kept on going—or I put bullet through him."

There were a few nervous chuckles at that. There was no doubt in the men's minds, obviously, that this woman they called Carlotta was quite capable of doing just what she had said she would do. Longarm counted his lucky stars she hadn't put a bullet in him when he first climbed into her room.

"You ain't seen him then?" persisted the second voice.

"How could I?" Carlotta replied tartly. "I was sleep-

23

ing until your men woke me. Now go way from here and look someplace else for thees man."

Without waiting for their response, she turned and slammed the door shut on them—then paused by the door, listening. Low mutters filtered through the door and open window as the men drifted off down the alley.

When the last of them was gone and the alley silent, she turned her head and looked at Longarm. "Wait a little while if you want—then leave me be. I need my sleep."

"They called you Carlotta."

"Yes."

"I'm Custis Long."

"My full name is Carlotta Red Wing. My mother was of Spanish blood, my father a full-blooded Apache."

"Looks like it made for a very beautiful combination."

His compliment, so easily and graciously given, caused her to blush. "You are very kind, señor."

"What do you do in this town?" he asked her.

"I run a boarding and rooming house with my aunt."

Longarm moved over to the door leading from the room and paused, his hand on the knob. "You didn't have to help me out like that. You put yourself out on a limb for me, and I'm grateful."

She moved closer to him, eyes glowing with an infectious warmth. "How grateful?"

He laughed at her impudence and said, "Careful. You tempt me."

"I will do so no more," she said, laughing softly. "It's late and I am very exhausted. I will show you out."

Lamp in hand, Carlotta opened the door for him and led the way into a roomy kitchen. Crossing it, she kept on past the dining room into a lamplit corridor leading to the front door. Under the stairs was a key rack, a bracket lamp fastened to the wall beside it.

"Where are you staying?" she asked Longarm as she paused by the door.

"The Palace Hotel."

"An ugly, dirty place."

"It sure as hell ain't 'The Finest Hotel South of Denver.'"

"We have one room left. If you want, I'll save it for you, and we have a room next to the kitchen and plenty of hot water if you want a bath." She smiled, her teeth brilliant in her dusky face. "We even have a tub big enough for you."

"You win," he said, grinning. "I'll check out of the Palace first thing in the morning and stop over here."

"I'll be looking forward to it, Mr. Long."

"Call me Custis."

She smiled and opened the door for him as he stepped out into the night.

Chapter 3

The next morning, Longarm arrived at Carlotta's boardinghouse well after breakfast. With most of the roomers and boarders off on their various occupations, Carlotta was able to give Longarm her complete attention, and after showing him to his room on the second floor, she reminded him of his expressed wish for a hot bath the night before.

She led him back downstairs to a room next to the kitchen, where five large, high-backed enamel tubs were kept for the boarders' use. While he undressed and changed into the bathrobe she provided, Carlotta and her aunt, Ventura, trooped steadily in from the kitchen with steaming buckets of hot water which they emptied into the largest of the tubs.

Then they left him to his hot bath. He stepped gingerly into the near-boiling water and lowered himself into it by tiny degrees until at last, sweat pouring off his forehead, the water lapped at his neck. He soaped himself down, and with a long-handled brush began scrubbing off the dust and grime of many miles. Occasionally, as he luxuriated in the hot, soapy water, Carlotta or Ventura would enter with a fresh bucket of steaming water, which they dumped into the tub in what Longarm thought might well be a playful attempt to scald him alive.

When he stepped from the tub, Carlotta appeared promptly on cue, and wrapping a large bath towel about him, patted him dry, a mischievous glint in her liquid eyes. Once or twice he felt her bare hand brush against his flanks, and she seemed to take a little more time than necessary patting him dry around his crotch—until Longarm found himself tingling all over. His mouth was dry with anticipation, his manhood on bold display when at last she tossed the towel over the back of a chair and, making no effort to avert her eyes, helped him into the robe.

"I will bring your clothes up later," Carlotta told him softly, her perfumed breath hot on the back of his neck. "Ventura is pressing your coat and pants. She say we need to wash your stockings and shirt too, maybe."

"Much obliged," he told her, and picking up his boots, he left the room and went upstairs.

He was in his long johns, unpacking a fresh shirt from his carpetbag, when a light rap came on his door. He pulled it open and Carlotta entered carrying his vest, pants, and frock coat. She was wearing a loose, blue silken housedress and from the way it followed the contours of her bosom and hips, nothing under it. The

28

dress's top four buttons were unbuttoned, the look in her eyes unmistakable. There was no way of misunderstanding her intent in coming up here at this moment to deliver his suit.

Without a word she placed his clothing, neatly folded, onto the top of his dresser, then turned to face him and proceeded to calmly unbutton her dress. Stepping out of his long johns, he watched for a moment as the lush fullness of her stood revealed in all its aching beauty—the strong, upthrusting breasts, the dusky swell of her belly, the black triangle, the flaring hips leading to the swell of her powerful thighs. Unable to contain his excitement any longer, he stepped close, bent, and swiftly undid the last button. Then, straightening, he pulled her long, supple nakedness hard against him, aware of the scalding urgency in his groin as his manhood thrusted eagerly, hungrily against her already moist warmth.

In a fever of impatience, he grabbed her thighs and lifted her up, then down onto his thrusting erection. She gasped and tightened her thighs about his waist as she flung her arms about his neck and clung to him, her lips closing about his. He turned and made for the bed, slamming down onto it with her under him. She gasped again as he drove deep into her, hitting bottom with his first stroke.

"Deeper, Custis!" she commanded.

Longarm did his best to oblige. He pulled out of her, leaving just the tip of his erection within her, then plunged deliberately, powerfully, deeper than he had been able to go before. Carlotta uttered a sharp, delighted cry that seemed to come from the deepest part of her. Her arms tightened convulsively around his neck as he continued to thrust and thrust again.

"That's it," she told him fiercely. "Keep going! Faster!"

After a dozen deep thrusts, Longarm felt her juices begin to flow. Her cries of excitement increased. With each shattering plunge her ecstasy mounted, her cries grew more intense, and it all had its effect on Longarm. He was also moving toward orgasm. He pounded harder, bringing sharp, deep yelps from Carlotta. Abruptly she became rigid under him. Her ankles tightened. Her inner muscles squeezed tightly about his erection, and he pressed hard for that instant before both of them came to a sudden, overwhelming outpouring.

Longarm fell forward onto Carlotta's glistening body, aware he was still large within her. She panted softly and straightened her legs out upon the bed and began to stroke his hair.

"Mmm," she said. "That was very good, Custis. Do you know how long it has been, Custis? In this damn town of drunken miners and unwashed cowpokes?"

"Long enough, I can guess."

"No, Custis. You can't imagine. This town is filled with men, all right. But they are either too dirty or too shy to know what a woman wants or how to give it to her. They understand it in animals, and in themselves—but not in a woman!"

She spoke passionately, angrily. Her frustration was like a hot wind that kept Longarm erect. He smiled down at her. "We kccp on talking like this, we're going to lose what I still got going down there inside you."

She smiled. "I can feel him! He's a wonder, truly he is, Custis. So eager!" He felt her tighten about him. "And so big! They say it is not important if a man is big. Don't you believe that, Custis."

"I won't, if you tell me not to."

30

With him still inside, she swung out from under him smoothly and mounted him from the top, falling forward heavily, gasping with pleasure as she felt him going in deeper and deeper. Soon their bodies were locked together and there was no room left for him to probe. Squeezing delightedly with the muscles in her buttocks, she began rotating her hips with delicious slowness.

Longarm lay back and let Carlotta have her way with him. She knew precisely how to prolong it as much as was humanly possible, pausing in her hip rotations more and more often, for shorter and shorter periods, as she succumbed to her own mounting pleasure. Abruptly, her long hair spilling down over Longarm's face and shoulders, she began rocking herself back and forth until at last, with a deep groan of joy, she poured her juices down over him in a hot, delicious explosion that sent her falling forward upon his chest, limp and trembling.

Longarm had held himself back for her, intent only on her pleasure. Now, keeping himself deep into her, he rolled over on top of her and began his own party.

"Oh!" she cried. "Again! So soon! I don't know if I can!"

"Sure you can," he said, chuckling. "Just lay back and let it happen."

He was already thrusting with full, slow, even strokes. He was determined not to hurry, and used only a part of his weight and strength. He had told her to lay back and relax, and that is just what she did for the first few minutes. She was still exhausted and panting from her own wildness a moment before, and at first it was obvious she was perfectly willing to lay back and let Longarm use her.

31

But gradually she found herself coming to life under him, and Longarm felt her inner muscles responding to his measured, metronomic thrusts. She began lifting her hips to meet them, but only slightly at first and just a few inches at a time. But then her face regained its rosy luster and he saw her breath sharpen, her eyes snapping open as she peered up at him with awakened interest—and need. She now met his thrusts openly and moved faster in order to lunge up at him with a kind of tough eagerness, as if this were some kind of battle they were engaged in. Sharp, tiny cries escaped from her. She began thrashing her head from side to side, as if she were in some kind of heavenly pain.

Meanwhile, Longarm was building to his own climax. It had been a long time coming—for both of them this time—but by now their bodies had achieved a fierce, violent unity. With mounting intensity, they slammed at each other with wonderfully controlled abandon. He pounded down into her now with fast, repeated thrusts until he could hear her sudden, sharp grunts. Abruptly she arched her back, thrusting up wildly as if she meant to throw him off, and he found he could hold back no longer and felt himself pulsing out of control, emptying, throbbing, until he was drained completely. His head swimming emptily, he dropped forward upon her, his chest resting against the incandescent warmth of her sweaty breasts, his face resting in the cloud of dark hair beside her cheek. He was spent completely.

When their breathing had quieted, Carlotta said softly, her fingers running idly through his hair, "That was nice, Custis. So very nice. Thank you."

"The feeling is mutual, Carlotta."

He rolled gently off her, but kept her in his arms. She

32

snuggled closer to him, their long naked bodies fitting perfectly, the top of her head thrust snugly under his chin. The sounds from the street came only dimly to them, since the room was in the back. But after a while its persistent clamor reminded Longarm that he was a working man, after all.

She felt him stiffen and pull away slightly, and pulled back herself to look at him. "Aren't you going to sleep? Most men do afterward."

He shook his head.

"Well, then, if you aren't completely spent, I'm sure I could . . ."

He laughed and shook his head. "I'm a working man —or will have to be soon, before my current stake runs out."

"What is your business, Custis—besides making *this* person feel a lot better, that is."

He shrugged. "Whatever comes handy, I guess."

"You're not a gunslick or a miner. I can tell that much. You a gambler, maybe?"

"Maybe. I've worked in saloons and I know how to play cards. Who's hiring men around here, anyway?"

"MacDuff, he say there is big turnover in teamsters that freight-out the ore. Not many of them can work long in that dust. It gets to their lungs, their eyes start to run, and they have to quit."

"Who's MacDuff?"

"One of the boarders. He is editor at the paper."

"I'm not much of a teamster, so I don't think I'll try that anyway. Any ranches around?"

"You don't look like a cowpuncher."

"Don't let that fool you. I punched my share of cows."

"Well, the cattlemen around here hire mostly Mexican hands. They work cheap, bring their families with them, and they are very loyal."

"So no footloose gringo need apply."

She smiled. "That is what I hear, Custis."

"Doesn't leave me much, does it."

"Well, there's one man might be able to help you—only from what I hear this morning about what you did last night in his saloon, you won't get much help from him. His name's Jim Gettis."

"Why should the owner of a saloon be a problem to me?"

"Because Jim Gettis does not own only Long Chance Saloon. He owns a ranch, two mines, the stamping mill and a general store. He or his men are probably out right now, looking for you. Anyone tangles with Gettis, he either leave town fast or stay here—in a pine box."

"I see."

She sat up and with a quick movement of her hand, brushed her hair back over her shoulder, then rested her back against the backboard. He elbowed himself closer and rested his head on her lap and peered up at her through the cleft in her breasts. She sighed contentedly.

"So you stay here," she told him, leaning forward and kissing him. "I will be sure to keep you busy."

"That wouldn't do, Carlotta. After all, what would Ventura say—or the other boarders?"

She laughed softly and ran her hand through his still-sweaty hair. "Ventura would not be a problem. She see you, she tell me I should be the one to make you happy. And these boarders, they do not have any right to tell me what to do. I give them room and board and feed them good. That is all Carlotta owe them."

"This man, Gettis. Do you know him?"

"I know him. I hate him very much, Custis, but he does not know this. I keep it to myself."

"You want to tell me about it?"

"I do not like to talk about it, Custis."

"You two on talking terms?"

She shrugged. "Of course. I am not such a fool as to let him know how I feel—or why. But I keep my distance."

"Would it be all right if I say you sent me?"

"You must be crazy. How will it matter to Jim Gettis that I send you? If you walk into that saloon after what you did to one of his men, he will maybe kill you—or let one of his men work you over." She shuddered. "I've seen how vicious his hired thugs can be."

"Maybe he'll go easy on me. After all, he should be glad I showed him what lousy bouncers he had on his payroll."

She shuddered. "I don't like it."

"Using your name will give me an opening. He'll be curious to see me if he knows I know you. I won't be just another roustabout coming in off the streets."

She smiled. "You could never be that, Custis. But you must be careful. He is a very terrible man. And it would be sad if you work for him and become like him."

Longarm reached up and rested the palm of his hand against her cheek. "Carlotta, if you'd rather not get involved, just say so."

She sighed. "Go ahead. I understand. A man must work. Even if it is for such an animal as Jim Gettis. Tell him I send you, if you want. It might not do you much good. If I were you, I'd watch my back."

"I'll do that," he promised.

"But first," she said, leaning over and closing her full lips about his, "we play some more, huh?"

For an answer, he pulled her down beside him.

Walking through the late morning heat, Longarm was aware of the thick curtain of dust already hanging in the still air above the street. A few ore carts rumbled past him, and a few horsemen galloped by, raising more dust. Wincing at the glare, Longarm ducked into the Long Chance Saloon and found it somewhat quieter than the night before. But that didn't mean it was empty. It was, in fact, doing a brisk business, considering the hour.

Skirting around a grizzled swamper, Longarm found an empty place at the bar and told the barkeep, "I'd like to see Mr. Gettis."

"That so?"

Longarm looked into the careless belligerence in the man's eyes and smiled. "Yes."

"He ain't come in yet," the barkeep replied grudgingly, his eyes wavering. "Be here in a half hour maybe."

Longarm nodded and returned to the street to wait— and maybe get a good look at Gettis while he was at it. He had no doubt Gettis would come in by the front. The owner of a saloon usually likes to tramp in first thing to check on the business the night before, make sure the place was being cleaned up, and any damages from the night before repaired.

The ore wagons traffic was getting heavier, the dust that hung over the street almost enough to screen out the sun's brutal rays. Almost. He straightened. Five riders had materialized through the screening dust. They were between two ore wagons and were headed directly for the saloon. Dressed in range clothes, they had all pulled their bandannas up to cover their mouths and noses from the dust. They were all armed, revolvers on their hips, carbines in their scabbards. The way they placed themselves as they rode—the two riders in front keeping abreast of each other, the single rider behind them, and two more bringing up the rear—made it pretty clear that the rider in the middle was the man being protected, and that he was afraid for his life.

The lone rider was obviously Paul Cable—or Jim Gettis, as he now called himself—and Longarm took a good look at the man. Gettis was a big man, heavy in the gut and shoulders.

The riders left the cover of the two ore wagons and rode for the tie rail in front of the Long Chance. The two lead riders, Gettis, and one of the two drag riders dismounted, while the fifth rider took the reins of the other horses and set off up the street to the livery stable. Leading his three bodyguards, Gettis strode through the break in the tie rail and brushed past Longarm without a sidelong glance, disappearing into the saloon. Longarm tugged his hat down to protect his eyes from the dust raised by the two passing ore wagons and ducked into the saloon behind Gettis and his bodyguards.

He saw Gettis and two of his guards disappearing into the back corridor Longarm had raced through to get to the alley the previous night. The third bodyguard had held back and now stood with his forearm resting on the bar. He was apparently keeping an eye on the door leading to the corridor.

Longarm angled through the patrons and came to a halt in front of him. He was a leathery, bleary-eyed

37

man, shorter than Longarm. He wore his gun strapped to his thigh and had the unmistakable smell of an ex-convict about him. He glared without comment at Longarm.

Longarm smiled casually. "Howdy," he said.

"What do you want, mister?"

"I want to see Mr. Gettis."

"He ain't here."

"That's funny. I just saw him go in that door."

"No you didn't."

Patiently, Longarm said, "Look, Shorty, I'll give you one more chance. Go back and tell your boss there's someone out here wants to see him. Tell him Miss Carlotta sent me."

The man straightened and hitched up his pants, his hand remaining down, his fingers hovering not far from the grips of his Colt revolver. "What if I don't?"

"I didn't come in here for trouble, Shorty. But I don't usually back away from it, either. Maybe you feel the same way."

"Guess maybe I do at that," said the bodyguard.

He pushed away from the bar and casually flipped aside Longarm's coat and lifted his Colt from the cross-draw rig. Then he stuck the revolver into his belt, turned, and vanished into the corridor. The barkeep walked down the bar to him. "What'll it be, mister?"

"Nothing," Longarm told him. "I'm waiting to see Mr. Gettis."

The bartender was about to turn away, but something in Longarm's eyes and manner reminded him of something. He seemed to tense, then straighten up, his eyes flicking quickly over Longarm's figure. Then, instead of going back up the bar, he moved on past Longarm, lifted the bar gate and vanished into the corridor.

Longarm understood. The barkeep remembered him from the night before.

Moments later, the guard reappeared in the doorway and beckoned to Longarm. As Longarm sidled past him in the doorway, the barkeep hurried past them both on his way back to the saloon. There was an air of importance about the man. He was obviously pleased with himself for recognizing Longarm and warning Jim Gettis. The bodyguard kept behind Longarm and told him to keep on going to the end of the corridor to a door on the right.

When Longarm reached it, the guard behind Longarm reached past him, turned the knob, and pushed the door open. Longarm entered, the guard trailing in after him and closing the door. The room was claustrophobic, the windows painted white for privacy, allowing for little more than an anemic, pale glow that fell over them like a deathly pallor. The two guards leaned back against the wall, watching Longarm with alert, feral interest—reminding him of waiting buzzards perched on a limb. The bodyguard who had brought Longarm in joined them.

Across the room was a large desk. Jim Gettis sat behind it. Longarm's .44 was resting on the desk in front of him. Seeing him closer now with his hat off, Longarm got a much clearer view of the man. Gettis had a large, powerful head set low and solidly into his hefty shoulders, giving an impression of tremendous solidity. He head was covered with kinky black hair. His broad Irish face held the scars of many a barroom scrap, and his short, powerful nose, after a series of beatings, now sat a little crookedly on his face. His wide mouth was thin-lipped and mobile, and at the moment it was close to breaking into a smile. Gettis was obviously

39

enjoying the irony of Longarm coming in to see him after so many of his men had spent the night scouring the town in a fruitless search for him.

But there was little genuine mirth in the man, and his green eyes, partially hidden under thick black brows, appraised Longarm as coldly as would a snake a moment before it struck. The man who now called himself Jim Gettis was no man to be taken lightly, Longarm realized—something the U.S. Army had long since found out.

"Morning, Mr. Gettis," Longarm said pleasantly enough.

Gettis nodded. "You said Miss Carlotta sent you."

"That she did."

"Why?"

"I'm lookin' for work and she said you had the most number of going enterprises in Copper City."

"You're looking for a job?"

"A man has to eat."

"You don't look like a miner or a prospector. Your hands are too soft."

Longarm shrugged.

"You think I should give a job to a man beat up one of my men?"

"Now, where'd you hear such a thing?"

"The barkeep recognized you, mister." Gettis leaned back in his chair and regarded Longarm thoughtfully. "I sure have to admit it, though. You got plenty of gall."

One of the three men standing against the wall laughed shortly, contemptuously. Gettis's look silenced him abruptly, then Gettis returned his full attention to Longarm.

"What was that business last night all about, mister?"

"I bought myself a beer and walked over to the faro

game to watch. The guard told me bet or move on. I didn't see that I was obstructing the play any, so I stayed put. Whistles started blowing and one of your bullyboys started to prod me."

"So you jammed in his nose with your stein and stuck the pool cue into his gut."

Longarm shrugged. "What you mean is one of your bouncers let me flatten his nose, then take his pool cue from him. I don't see as I had much choice, Mr. Gettis, and I don't see that you should be very proud of your hired man. He didn't do so well."

Another snort came from the wall, But Gettis silenced the man responsible with a quick, angry glance, then smiled coldly back at Longarm. "You don't think much of my men. That it?"

"I just came in for a beer, Mr. Gettis. Your men sure didn't make me feel welcome. Seems like that's a helluva way to run a saloon. Picking on the customers."

"Maybe you got a point there, mister. But I got a man in bed with a broken nose, and he can't stand up to pee. You think I should stand still for that?"

Longarm shrugged. "If it makes you shorthanded, maybe I can take that feller's place."

A derisive bark came from two of the three men along the wall and Gettis leaned back in his chair once more, obviously amused. "I don't even know your name," he said.

"Custis Long."

Gettis glanced over at the biggest of the three men and nodded. The big man took off his shell belt, and then unbuckled the wide belt holding up his trousers. Then he wrapped the belt around the palm of his right hand. The other two left the wall and moved around behind Longarm. Longarm knew what they had in

41

mind. Two of them would haul him out into the alley and hold him while the man with the belt-wrapped fist beat his face to a pulp.

Longarm looked at Gettis. "If they are going to do what I think they're going to do, the man with the strap is as good as dead," he said matter-of-factly. "If not now, some time later. He can bank on it."

Gettis tipped his head slightly and let his green eyes gaze deep into Longarm's—as if he were looking into the man's soul in an effort to gauge his resolve. "Suppose Mac kills you, Long?"

"Of course, that's different," Longarm replied easily. "And that's just what he'll have to do if he wants to live."

Gettis laughed, somewhat nervously. "And what about me?"

"I figure the host of the feast is always responsible if a guest dies of food poisoning."

Gettis seemed satisfied that Longarm meant what he said, and that he was not just bluffing. He looked sharply at the three men. "Pull back, boys. I think the son of a bitch means it—unless you want to find out for sure, Mac."

Mac pulled up, hesitant. His enthusiasm had drained away at Longarm's cold, matter-of-fact statement. Longarm had not raised his voice, nor seemed in the slightest bit cowed by the odds against him. And all three knew about the bouncer Longarm had dealt with the previous night. Gettis laughed to break the tension. Then he picked Longarm's gun off his desk and tossed it to him.

"See Johnny Calder before four this afternoon," he

told Longarm. "He runs the place. I'll tell him to expect you."

Longarm dropped the Colt into his holster and buttoned his coat. "Much obliged for the job, Mr. Gettis."

Then he turned and left the room.

Chapter 4

When Longarm returned to the boardinghouse, he asked Ventura for Carlotta and was told she was in the kitchen. He entered the kitchen and found Carlotta cleaning off the top of the large black stove.

"Well?" she said. "Did Gettis give you a job?"

"He did."

She turned completely around to face him, her face registering something very close to shock. It was clear she had not expected for a single moment that Longarm would be able to get a job from Jim Gettis. "What will you do for him?"

"I'm his new bouncer in the Long Chance. Seems that gent I tangled with last night is in no condition to do his job properly."

"That is not very nice job, Custis. Now you must beat the heads of poor drunk miners."

"I can keep order without going that far."

"Maybe," she said doubtfully. "You are sure big enough, but them Long Chance housemen are very much hated. They have to walk through town in pairs and carry guns. If any miners catch one of them alone, they will keel heem." She shrugged, still perplexed. "I tell you I still cannot believe it. I am so surprise. I cannot think why Jim Gettis will give you a job in his saloon after you hurt his man so bad."

Longarm grinned. "Good sense prevailed, I guess."

She turned back to the stove and reached for a steaming coffeepot. "Sit down. I have just now make fresh coffee."

Longarm slumped at the small table near the window as Carlotta filled their cups. As soon as she sat down across from him, Longarm sipped the black coffee and said, "Jim Gettis struts around like he owns this town, Carlotta."

Her voice filled with scorn, she said, "He does own it."

"Now how in hell did he manage that?"

"When he ride into this town, he have many tough gunslicks at his back. He close down all the gambling houses and saloons. Now his saloon is the only one, except the hotel saloon."

"You make it sound easy."

"For this man, it was. His toughs stage big fights in a saloon. They wreck it, break windows, mirrors, chairs, tables—and even the bar. When the saloons, they were built again, Gettis's men would make another fight and wreck the place all over again. Many of these saloon owners complain to the deputy sheriff, but he is paid by Gettis, so he do nothing. At last, the saloon owners

46

understand they are helpless, so they leave town. Now he has only saloon in Copper City."

"Except for the saloon in the hotel, you said."

She shrugged and sipped her coffee. "What does he care about businessmen and travelers? He wants the miners because they are so stupid they think his rotten whiskey is fine and they lose all their money at his crooked gaming tables. And if they complain, his housemen beat them up."

"I see."

"It is not very pretty, no? And now you work for him."

"He can't make me do anything I don't want to do. That's a promise, Carlotta."

"It does not matter to me," she told him. "It is your soul to lose. I am not responsible."

He could sense her distancing herself from him. It saddened him, but he knew there was nothing he could do about it. He thanked her for the coffee and left the boardinghouse to see his new boss, Johnny Calder, the man who ran the saloon for Gettis.

Calder's office was across the corridor from Gettis's. Longarm knocked on the door and a man's voice told him to come in.

Longarm pushed open the door and entered the small room. The blonde faro dealer called Casey was sitting in a chair beside a flat counting table. Nodding politely to her, Longarm swept off his hat. At the table, his back to the window, sat the manager of the saloon, Johnny Calder. In front of him on the table were numerous stacks of gold and silver coins.

Turning his head, Calder said, "Who the hell're you?"

It was Casey who answered for Longarm. "He's the one taking Mick's place. His name is Long. As a matter of fact," Casey added, an ironic smile on her face, "he's the one who broke Mick's own cue stick over his head."

Calder turned completely about in his chair then to view Longarm more closely. He was a pale, gaunt, scarecrow of a man with sunken cheeks and eyes that blazed with a hectic, consumptive light. His hands resting on the counting table were like great claws. He surveyed Longarm coldly, his eyes measuring Longarm's six feet of heavy bone and hard muscle with a mixture of resentment and envy.

"Sit down," he told Longarm, nodding toward a straight-backed chair on Longarm's left. Then he added, "You think you got the stomach for this job?"

"Ask Mick," Longarm replied, sitting down and crossing his legs.

"First thing is get yourself some white shirts. That's what you'll be wearing."

"Why?"

"So you can spot the other housemen in a hurry, and so they can see you when you start to mix it up. These damned miners sure as hell don't wear white shirts, so you'll stand out."

Both he and Casey chuckled at that.

"Just what is my job?"

"You mean you don't know? Break up fights. Keep the peace. That's a goddamn bear pit out there, or didn't you notice that?"

"Do I pack a gun?"

"Not in that mob. It'd be too easy to lift it off you. You'll be packing a sawed-off pool cue, instead. And don't be afraid to use it. These miners have thick skulls, and the cue sticks tend to slip off them wool hats they

48

use. You better be ready to give them a real belt."

"I saw him at work last night," Casey said to Calder. "He's got the muscle for it." As she spoke, she glanced at Longarm with some respect—even admiration—in her eyes.

Calder shrugged. "Okay. So you know how to take care of yourself. But your main job is to keep an eye on Casey. These bohunks haven't seen a real woman in a long time. The only females they been plowin' keep their boots on in bed and a hair full of graybacks. We figure these hunkies and micks play faro just to get close to Casey. So you got to see to it that they don't get too close. They tend to get carried away after that rotgut hits their bellies."

Longarm glanced at Casey. He could understand the miners' dilemma. She was an awful lot of woman, almost too much for the comprehension of these ill-used, filthy miners. Looking up at him, Casey smiled, as if she could read his thoughts.

"Watch Sloan, Long," she told him. "He's the guard with the shotgun. He's got a whistle. When he let's go, you come running. If I see trouble coming, I just do this."

She lifted her right hand and placed her fingers against the hollow in her throat.

"Just watch for that signal," said Calder. "Anything else you want to know?"

"Nope. Thanks, Calder."

"Mr. Calder to you, Long. You're working for me as well as Jim Gettis. Don't forget that."

Longarm stood up and nodded obediently. "Yes, sir, Mr. Calder."

Somehow, despite his response and the polite nod that accompanied it, Longarm did not give either of them the impression that he was properly impressed by Calder. Quite the opposite. Smiling, Casey got to her feet and smoothed out her green skirt.

"Nice to meet you, Mr. Long," she said, moving past him to the door, the rustle of her silk filling the small room.

As soon as she was gone, Longarm looked back down at the cadaverous manager and asked, "What would make a woman like that work in such a foul bear pit as the Long Chance?"

"She's Jim Gettis's woman."

"Oh?"

"And you better not forget that, mister. Now maybe you better go get them white shirts. I got some countin' to do."

Longarm put his hat back on, turned, and left.

Dressed in one of his new clean white shirts and minus his vest and frock coat, Longarm pushed into the Long Chance a little before six that evening. Moving through the crush, he reached the bar and beckoned to the same barkeep who had recognized him the day before.

"I'll be working here from now on," Longarm told him.

"I heard," the barkeep said, apparently not all that enthusiastic about the idea.

But he said nothing further. Reaching under the bar, he brought up an assortment of sawed-off pool cues and laid them down on the top of the bar for Longarm's inspection. The first thing Longarm noticed was that some of them had wrist thongs. Longarm quickly decided not to bother with those. One snatch of his club could maybe wrench his arm out of its socket, he realized. He tried two of the cues without thongs and selected the one whose heft he felt comfortable with, then asked for some Maryland rye.

Leaning back against the bar, he looked the saloon over. A dealer and case tender were setting up Casey's faro layout. She was wearing a white silk blouse this time, and already a few men were drifting over to her table. Another bouncer stood a few feet from her, watching idly, his pool cue stuck in his belt. He was big enough, Longarm realized, and his face was as battered as an old barn door hanging on one leather hinge. Two other housemen were slowly cruising about the saloon, stopping every now and then to chat with acquaintances. The mines hadn't disgorged the day shift yet; these few quiet moments were the calm before the storm.

Longarm had taken a couple of pulls on his rye when one of the white-shirted bouncers passed close by him, ignoring him completely. The other housemen were also ignoring him, doing all they could to pretend he was not really a part of their operation. He could understand their attitude. After all, he had put one of their number in bed and then taken his job. It was not exactly the best way to make friends. The thing was, in a pinch, Longarm was going to have to count on them to come to his aid.

Longarm finished his drink. The fifth houseman came out of the back corridor and surveyed the slowly filling saloon. His glance fell momentarily on Longarm, then slid past without a nod or acknowledgment of his presence. No question about it. The four other bouncers were prepared to ignore him completely. In a pinch Longarm would have to count on only one man—himself.

His pool cue tucked into his belt, Longarm began to move about the room. At the same time the shotgun-toting guard took his place on the chair beside Casey's faro table. Now, as the miners and teamsters drifted into the saloon, the townsmen finished their drinks and left.

One of the bouncers began lighting the pull-down lamps over the faro and poker tables. To keep himself busy, Longarm lit a few as well and even as he finished, the miners began pouring into the place, the level of noise rising with almost menacing swiftness. Before long there were ranks three-men deep at the bars, and as Longarm cruised the length of the bar, he passed one of the other housemen going in the opposite direction. Neither one of them acknowledged the presence of the other.

The first ruckus of the night erupted about an hour later. Longarm was closest. Two miners at the far end of the bar were shouting at each other, the air hot with their curses, and they made no effort to calm down as those close beside them tried to pull them apart. A hand lashed out, and Longarm heard the smack of a fist slamming into a cheek. At once the two men squared away. Longarm moved in swiftly, put an arm under the arm of each of them and slowly but firmly marched them through the crush of miners and out the door. Once outside in the darkened street, the miners flung themselves away from Longarm and began pummeling each other with such drunken clumsiness that their efforts brought first derisive laughter, then indifference.

Longarm returned to the saloon, and this time moved toward Casey's table, remembering that he was expected to do his part in keeping obstreperous miners out of her hair. As he halted beside Sloan's chair, the fellow moved his shotgun nervously and frowned up at him.

"Ain't you the son-of-a-bitch started that fight last night?" he demanded, his beefy face growing suddenly red. "What in hell you doin' wearing a white shirt?"

Casey overheard him. Without looking up, she said, "Ease off, Sloan. He works here. Jim hired him this morning."

Longarm grinned at Sloan, then moved away, heading toward the bar through the growing reek of whiskey, tobacco smoke, chewing tobacco, and the awful stench of unwashed feet and sweating bodies. Shoving past a bearded miner, he felt his arm grabbed. He turned to see a big, blocky miner with a thick black beard straightening to send a fist into his face. Throwing up his forearm, Longarm blocked the punch just as another man lunged at him from behind, grabbing both his arms. Whoever held him was strong enough, and Longarm's first impulse was to backpedal quickly.

He did so and the fellow went down under him. As Longarm landed hard on the fellow, he heard the man gasp as the air was expelled from his lungs. Rolling off the fellow, he leaped to his feet and reached for his cue stick. It was gone, having already slipped to the floor. Grimly, he went after the man who had thrown the punch at him. The fellow drove a looping blow at his face. Longarm ducked. The blow slammed off his skull. The miner howled as his fist felt the impact. Longarm lunged closer and drove his knee into the miner's groin and heard a bellow of pain as the miner jackknifed over.

Again Longarm's knee shot up, this time slamming into the miner's bearded face. But the other miner was on his feet again. From behind, he wrapped both arms around Longarm, burying his chin in the back of Longarm's neck. As he squeezed hard in an effort to immobilize Longarm, Longarm lifted a leg and stomped his heel viciously back and down on the miner's foot. There was a grunt of pain and the fellow released Longarm and reached down for his injured foot.

Flinging around, Longarm brought his fist down on the back of the miner's neck and saw him go down like a felled ox. Glancing up then, wondering where the other bouncers were, Longarm glimpsed one of the white-shirted bouncers standing at the bar, calmly watching the fight. He appeared to be immensely enjoying the spectacle of Longarm trying to fight off two attackers at once.

As Longarm swung back to the other miner, his foot struck his pool cue. Reaching down swiftly, he brought it up just in time to bounce it off the bearded miner's skull. The fellow went down on one knee. Longarm stepped back and kicked him in the face. The miner's head snapped back and his whole body flipped over, just as the other one revived enough to hurl himself at Longarm, catching him in the small of the back. Grunting with the exertion, he propelled Longarm swiftly across the floor ahead of him. Longarm saw the ring of grinning onlookers part swiftly to make way for him.

Still hanging on to his sawed-off cue stick, Longarm slammed hard against the side of a table and drove it ahead of him through the sawdust for a few feet before its legs gave way. As the edge of the table bit into the floor, Longarm went sailing over it, his assailant following clumsily after him. Both men struck the floor within a few feet of each other. On his knees in an instant, Longarm brought his cue stick around and caught the miner on the side of his jaw. The sickening sound of his jawbone snapping was clearly audible to those miners crowding around. Grabbing his shattered jaw, the miner looked up at Longarm, his tearing eyes pleading for an end to any further punishment.

54

Scrambling to his feet, Longarm stuck his cue stick into his belt and, grabbing the back of the man's filthy shirt, dragged him from the saloon and dumped him into the street. When he went back for the other one, he found him gone from the place, an awed crowd of miners drifting cautiously away from him rather than meet his aroused glare.

The four bouncers stood alone now at various spots about the saloon. Not a single one had made any effort to come to Longarm's aid. It was obvious to everyone in the place that the four housemen had put those two miners up to the attack on Longarm, and now the miners and teamsters watched eagerly for Longarm's response to their treachery. They had seen one wild, wicked, no-holds-barred brawl. Were they going to see another one, they wondered as they saw the anger—and the contempt—in Longarm's face as he regarded the four men. Longarm could sense that these miners, no matter how much they hated the bouncers Gettis had hired to keep them in line, were on his side in this one.

In the waiting silence, Longarm addressed the four men. "Thanks, you bastards," he drawled. "You were a great help. How much did you pay those two to come after me?"

"Watch your mouth," said one of the men, a bald fellow with a heavy gut and small, mean eyes.

Longarm looked at him. "Whatever you paid them, it wasn't enough."

"I said shut up."

"You want to shut me up?"

The man pulled back and looked at his fellow bouncers. When they made no effort to back his play, he said heavily, "Maybe not now, mister. But your time will come. Putting on that white shirt don't make you one of us."

"That so? Maybe Jim Gettis will have something to say about that."

The four men glanced unhappily at each other, looking like kids caught with their fists in a cookie jar. Any immediate threat from them had passed for the moment, Longarm realized. He squared his shoulders, aware that his right shoulder, the one that had cushioned his fall over the table, ached smartly. His shirt was torn and streaked with tobacco juice and sawdust. There was a washroom at the end of the back corridor, and Longarm headed for it, eager to clean off his shirt as much as he could.

As he walked the length of the bar, the miners crowded around him, some cheering, others slapping him heartily on the back. A few offered him a drink. For this moment at least, they were on his side. He had given them a fight they would be talking about for some time—even if it was against some of their own. Watching one man overcome two-to-one odds in a knockdown-drag-out battle was a sight to warm the cockles of their hearts.

When he returned to the saloon, he continued to cruise the place, fully aware now that he could count on no help at all from the other bouncers. As he moved about, he was careful to keep his back protected, but the miners seemed predisposed to make it easy for him, and there were no more fights or even loud altercations for the remainder of that night. At closing, he left the place and walked to Carlotta's boardinghouse and let himself in.

In his room, he sacked out fully clothed on the bed and stared up at the ceiling, considering his position. He couldn't see how his working for Gettis as a bouncer was bringing him any closer to accomplishing his mission, which was to bring a renegade sergeant back in chains to face an army court-martial. Still, it was too early for him to get anxious. He was now part of Gettis's operation. That much he had accomplished. He would just have to play his cards close to his vest and wait for his chance. There was even a chance that this night's business might work in his favor.

Time would tell.

He got up and undressed, thinking of Carlotta. She must have heard him come in, he realized. He had expected to hear her rap softly on his door any minute to ask how things had gone. But he finished undressing and slipped under the covers without any rap on his door to interrupt him. He realized then that Carlotta had lost some of her enthusiasm for Custis Long.

Now that he was on Jim Gettis's payroll.

Chapter 5

Longarm slept late the next morning and left the boardinghouse without seeing Carlotta. He rented a horse at the livery stable, and while the Mexican hostler saddled up the black he had selected, he asked as casually as he could the whereabouts of Jim Gettis's cattle ranch. The Mexican told him that Gettis's Circle G ranch lay some sixteen miles south of Copper City, close by the border.

Under a cloudless blue sky, Longarm headed south through a barren wasteland of rock and sand, yucca, and mesquite baking in the sun. The bunchgrass was so sparse that Longarm found it hard to believe that any local cattlemen could graze much more than a single cow for every three hundred acres. As his black plodded on through the sun-scoured landscape he saw an occasional jackrabbit, and against the high blue sky, vultures drifting like cinders as they searched the stove top below for nourishment.

An hour out of Copper City Longarm saw a patch of dust hovering above the horizon. Pulling up, he narrowed his eyes and peered patiently into the cloud. Riders. He estimated four, maybe five. He cut into the oven-hot protection of a canyon, dismounted and led his horse out of sight, then returned to the mouth of the canyon to wait for the riders to move on past him. He figured they might well be riders from Gettis's ranch, and he didn't want to meet them and have to explain what he was doing out here.

When they had ridden past, the dust of their passage sitting on the horizon, he mounted up, left the canyon, and continued south. The country lifted noticeably about a mile beyond the canyon. It was still desert, but less barren. He began to spot cattle. They were rangy longhorns and spooked like deer when he came close. A half hour or so later, he reached a ridge and followed it almost straight south and soon glimpsed a line of pure green foliage far ahead of him. He rode on, came to a patch of rimrock, dismounted, and led his horse to the edge of the ridge.

Below him was a green valley. Its fields were irrigated, and less than a mile from where he crouched there was a large, single-story adobe ranch house. Between it and the irrigated fields were the corrals and outbuildings and the horse pasture. At least twenty head were grazing in it. From the base of the rimrock, a creek flowed past the ranch house through the horse pasture, and into the elaborate network of ditches that irrigated the distant fields.

This must be Jim Gettis's Circle G. It was the creek that made this all possible, transforming this portion of the desert into a virtual Eden. Gettis must have had to pay dearly, not only to build this irrigation system, but also to buy out a half-dozen families and their water rights. Only a man who had just stolen an army payroll would have that kind of money in his possession.

He had found the renegade sergeant, all right. There could no longer be any doubt—if there ever had been—that Jim Gettis and Sergeant Paul Cable were one and the same.

Mounting up, Longarm headed back to Copper City.

There were less than a dozen customers in the Long Chance. The faro layouts were idle, and only a couple of poker games were in progress. As Longarm walked the length of the bar, he noticed that two of the barkeeps regarded him somewhat sullenly. He was, in their eyes, still the man who had beaten up Mick and taken his job, an interloper they were not yet willing to accept as a friend.

Longarm ignored them in turn, walked through the doorway and down the corridor toward Calder's office. The door leading out onto the back alley was opened, planting a bright beam of light onto one wall. By its light Longarm saw one of Gettis's bodyguards stationed outside Calder's office. The door was open. Longarm nodded to the bodyguard, and before he could knock, Calder waved him in.

Stepping in past the guard, Longarm saw Jim Gettis sitting on the edge of Calder's counting table, neat ranks of tied sacks of coins on the table beside him. Gettis nodded to Longarm in greeting.

"Saw you ride out this morning," Calder noted, leaning back in his swivel chair.

"I needed the change—after last night."

61

Calder chuckled. "I heard about that battle you had. So did Jim here. You don't look none the worse for it."

Longarm took off his hat and slumped down into a straight-backed chair along the wall and shrugged. "It wasn't me got hurt."

"So I understand," said Gettis. "This morning, Casey told me you had to handle two miners alone—that you got no help from the other housemen. That right?"

"That's about the size of it."

"Why the hell would they do that?"

"Well, first off, they paid the two miners to go after me. That's the way I see it."

Gettis frowned, considering Longarm's accusation. Then he nodded. "Makes sense, I guess. They wanted to get back at you for putting Mick out of commission."

"That's the way I see it too, Jim," said Calder.

"Those bastards," muttered Gettis. "Who the hell do they think they're working for? Me or themselves?"

"They've been acting a mite independent of late," Calder noted, "from what Casey's been telling me."

"Yeah. So I hear." Gettis looked back at Longarm, his eyes narrowing shrewdly. "I understand you took care of both miners—without any help. You left one all broken up outside the saloon, and the other one ran out the back. You sure as hell know how to handle yourself, Long."

Longarm shrugged. "What choice do I have?"

With surprising warmth, Gettis smiled, then stuck out his powerful ham of a hand. "Shake," he said. "When I got my back to the wall, that's when I fight the hardest. I understand perfectly. I got a feeling you and me together could take on this whole town if we had a mind—with just our fists."

Longarm grinned back. "Maybe, but I'd hate like

hell to try that right now. Give me time to rest up."

Gettis laughed outright, then turned to Calder. "Pay them four bastards off, every last one of them—and don't forget to tell them why."

"Sloan, too?"

"No. His job is to stick close by Casey. He does that fine, Casey says. It's them housemen I want out of here. Then get me some hungry miners who're tired of blasting muck underground. They might like the idea of working in white shirts. Get on it fast. I want the new crew in here for tonight."

As Calder got to his feet and moved quickly past Longarm, Longarm said to Gettis, "Isn't that a bit drastic? I can understand how the housemen felt when they saw me taking their buddy's place."

"Sure. I can understand it, too. But that don't mean I have to stand still for it. Like I told Johnny, they work for me—or they don't work at all." His expression softened. "How'd you like to chuck that white shirt, Long?"

"For what?"

"I'm not sure yet. But I'd like to be able to count on you. You stand tall when you have to, and you got balls. A man like you is a comfort to have around—especially for a man like me."

"Then I'm still on your payroll?"

Gettis nodded. "And your salary is doubled. When you eat at Stella's, don't pick up the tab. That'll be on me, too."

"Will I still get such fine service?"

Gettis grinned. "Hell, you'll get a hundred percent better when I finish talking to Stella."

Longarm stood up and clapped his hat on. "Thanks, Mr. Gettis."

"Hell, Custis," Gettis protested good-naturedly, "call me Jim."

Longarm nodded, said good-bye, and went out past the lookout. It was noon, so Longarm stopped at the bar and purchased a bottle of Maryland rye to go with anything Carlotta might have left over in the kitchen. Then he left the Long Chance and headed for the boarding-house.

A moment later, the guard outside Gettis's office door poked his head in. "Kincaid's out here. He wants to see you."

Gettis was behind the desk in Calder's swivel chair, busy counting the sacks of gold and entering the amounts in his huge ledger. Looking up, he frowned and closed the ledger. He nodded to the bodyguard.

"Send him in."

The deputy sheriff strode in and slumped into the straight-backed chair beside the desk. Taking off his hat, Kincaid mopped his brow with a polka-dot kerchief and grinned slyly at Gettis.

"Hot as the hinges of hell out there," he said. "That's a great idea of yours, Jim—painting these windows to keep out the glare."

Gettis nodded, but said nothing in reply. Kincaid had an air about him that warned Gettis that Bull Kincaid was feeling his oats and was about ready to take him on. Gettis was not surprised. Kincaid was greedy and Gettis had known it would only be a matter of time before the man overreached himself.

Leaning back in his chair, Gettis tipped his head. "What do you want, Bull?"

"Just thought I'd drop in, Jim."

"Don't give me that horseshit, Bull. That ain't why

you stopped in here. You got a look about you. Like a vulture has when it's gettin' ready to drop on a carcass. Out with it."

Kincaid stirred uneasily on his seat. It was unnerving to have himself read so easily. He took out his kerchief again and mopped his brow. "Hell, Jim, there ain't no reason for you to get your bowels in an uproar."

Gettis sighed. "Look, Bull, I'm busy. I got work to do. If all you came in here for was to shoot the shit, get out. My time is valuable."

Kincaid sat up in his chair and moistened his suddenly dry lips. It was clear to Gettis that from Bull's standpoint, nothing seemed to be going the way he had rehearsed it in his mind. Gettis almost smiled.

"All right, Jim. All right. I was goin' to wait till you had more time, but I guess I might as well speak my piece now, while I'm here."

Sitting up in his chair, Gettis smiled, his square face almost kindly as he regarded Kincaid. "Then do it. Like I said, I'm busy."

"It's about my girls, Jim."

"I figured that."

"Jim, I know we been over this before, but it ain't fair—you keepin' my girls out of here. They ain't makin' shit in those cribs south of town. If you'd let them in here, where the men could get a good look at them, maybe buy them a drink, they'd double their take."

"And you'd double your take."

"Sure. What's wrong with that? I'd cut you in."

"That's right generous of you."

"Come on, Jim. I'm serious about this."

"I can see you are," Gettis acknowledged coldly, his gaze hard. "How many times do I have to tell you, Bull.

65

There's only one woman in the Long Chance. Casey. You run the whores south of town, and I'll run the games and booze."

Kincaid shook his head stubbornly. "Damn it, Jim. That ain't good enough."

"Then ride out."

"No."

"What you got in mind, Bull?"

"Building my own saloon and runnin' my girls upstairs."

So that was it. Gettis had wondered what Kincaid was up to. There had been talk about him being restless, and all of the talk had gotten back to Gettis. The deputy sheriff liked to drink and talk at the same time. A dangerous, foolish habit.

When Gettis did not respond, Kincaid added hastily, "I'll cut you in for half, Jim. I ain't greedy."

"You won't cut me in, Bull, because there's not going to be any saloon in town with girls. Your girls or mine."

"What the hell's got into you, Jim? You got something against girls? Hell, you're livin' with one right now—you can take her whenever you want to. Other men need a woman now and then, too. Why not make money on them?"

Gettis got to his feet and walked out from behind the desk, his gaze smoldering as he looked down at Kincaid. In that instant the deputy sheriff realized he had blundered grievously in bringing Casey into this discussion—especially in tying her in with his own whores. He should have bit his tongue first.

Gettis reached down and grabbed Kincaid's front collar and hauled him roughly upright. Then he spun him around and planted a solid kick on his big ass and sent him hurtling out through the open door and headfirst into the wall across the corridor. Following him out the door, Gettis watched as the man slumped dazedly to the corridor's floor and blinked miserably up at Gettis.

Gettis turned to his bodyguard. "Get Slim and Shorty. I want this asshole out of here—on the run."

A moment later, with Gettis following behind them to watch, his three bodyguards half carried, half dragged the deputy sheriff out of the corridor and through the saloon, after which they propelled him out through the batwings with such force he slammed belly-down over the hitch rack. His weight caused the rack to snap like a gunshot, and when he hit the dust of the street, every eye within a block was on him as he rolled over in the dust, blinking miserably up at the growing ring of grinning faces staring down at him.

Deputy Sheriff Bull Kincaid was not a popular man in Copper City, and his comeuppance was enjoyed hugely by those townsmen and miners watching him paw around for his hat, then struggle groggily to his feet and go stumbling off down the street toward his office.

Gettis moved back inside the saloon and once inside his office, he closed the door, put his feet up on the desk and tipped his hat down over his forehead to keep out the glare that pushed through the painted windows. Anger was still hammering in his temples. He was not afraid of Kincaid going for the sheriff in Travis, better than fifty miles northeast. He didn't have a leg to stand on, once Gettis pointed out to the sheriff that Kincaid was running a string of girls on the side. If that got out, he'd just be another saddle tramp looking for work. No, Kincaid would keep his mouth shut. He had no alternative.

But he was still trouble. He could still go ahead and build his own saloon in defiance of Gettis. He'd been shaking down his girls for long enough to have quite a pile by now. That he wanted Gettis to go in with him only meant that he was too cheap to put up all the money himself. That might change, however.

And once Kincaid got himself an operation, he'd have enough money to expand—and maybe import hardcases of his own to go against Gettis's men. That must not be allowed.

Kincaid would have to be stopped at all costs.

Passing the offices of the *Banner,* the town's weekly newspaper, Longarm almost ran over MacDuff as the editor stepped out onto the sidewalk. The man was on his lunch hour, it appeared. MacDuff also boarded at Carlotta's, and Carlotta had introduced them. At sight of Longarm, the pudgy, pink-cheeked editor brightened.

"Aha," he cried, "the brawler extraordinaire, is it?"

Pulling up, Longarm nodded. "Hello, MacDuff."

"Is that a bottle in your hand, sir?"

"It is."

"Rotgut or the genuine article?"

"Maryland rye."

"I am not hungry, but in this dust bowl I have a huge thirst. I suggest we go somewhere quiet where we may investigate more thoroughly the glories of that vintage."

"My room?"

"Excellent suggestion, my good man. Excellent."

A moment later, as the two men entered the boardinghouse, they spotted Carlotta coming down the stairs toward them, a dust mop in her hand, a kerchief wrapped about her hair. She greeted MacDuff amiably enough, but her manner as she greeted Longarm was subdued, even perplexed. At that moment Longarm cursed the editor's presence. He would have liked to have made use of this opportunity to thaw Carlotta. But she did not pause as she swept past them and vanished into the kitchen, and the moment was lost.

In his room, Longarm pulled two chairs over to the window, and as he and MacDuff sat down, he pulled the commode over to let it serve as a table. He filled their glasses about halfway, then, after a cordial salute, took a healthy belt and sat back, asking MacDuff how Jim Gettis had been able to acquire that lush green ranchland Longarm had glimpsed south of town.

"You tryin' to figure out what kind of animal that man is?"

"He's treated me decent. I'm curious about him, is all."

"You better be more than curious. He's a dangerous man."

"So Carlotta told me."

"That's a sweet and lovely woman. You listen to her, you won't go wrong."

"Since I've tied in with Gettis, she ain't said much to me."

MacDuff nodded, as if he understood perfectly, and took another gulp of the rye. His halo-like cloud of white hair made him look almost angelic. "Now *that's* a loss, lad. If I were you, I'd dump Gettis and concentrate on Carlotta. She's a damn sight prettier."

"I need the job, MacDuff."

The editor sighed. "I guess I can understand that. We all of us have to work for a living—even if it means shaking hands with the devil."

The devil, Longarm realized, was a reference to Jim Gettis. "Tell me about this devil, MacDuff. How'd

Gettis come to be so powerful? Where'd he come from?"

"The same place we all come from, lad—a checkered past. The word is he rode in one day leading six hardcases. He looked around until he found that valley with the creek watering it. There were six or seven Mexican families farming there and running some sheep." MacDuff took another gulp of his drink, then wiped his mouth. "He took that valley like Caesar taking Gaul. First he destroyed their crops, then, by God, he laid siege to their adobes, one by one. He'd attack a place at night and he never left a survivor, man, woman, or child. After the third massacre, the rest of the Mexicans pulled up stakes and went back to Mexico."

"What about the law?"

"What law there was, was busy with claim jumpers and shootings in town here. Hell, nobody knew those Mexicans existed—or cared. I don't reckon the Mexicans ever realized they were in the U.S. They just ran and Gettis took over their land."

"Where'd Gettis get his mine? I understand he has one."

"He has that. He staked two brothers for a half interest in whatever they came up with, and when they hit pay dirt, Gettis had his men pick a fight with them. When the smoke cleared, the brothers were dead, and Gettis was left with their claim. It is one of the best mines in them hills, almost as much silver as copper."

"The brothers had no family?"

"Who knows, Custis. This furnace of a town is populated by men who have only faces and names—no history."

Sipping his drink, Longarm nodded.

MacDuff finished his drink, and when Longarm reached for the bottle to refill his glass, the editor waved him off and got unsteadily to his feet. He blinked his eyes at Longarm, then winked. His pink face was flushed almost scarlet. It was obvious he was feeling no pain.

"Thanks for the booze," the editor said. "It ain't often I get a chance to drink my lunch. I'm much obliged."

Longarm went with him to the door and watched as the man descended the steps on his unsteady legs, his left hand clutching the railing. He made it to the door without untoward incident and Longarm heard the front door slam as the editor left. He closed the door to his room and flopped down on his bed. Folding his arms under his head, he stared up at the crack in his ceiling, going over in his mind what he had learned from MacDuff.

The editor had not told him much he didn't already know. What he had done was fill in a few blank spots for Longarm. The picture he now had of Jim Gettis was pretty clear—and sobering. This land was populated by renegades and gunslicks, most of them with a past and few with a place they could ever call home. And Gettis was no different. Like his men, no doubt, he had long since burned all his bridges. He was a cruel man keeping himself alive in a cruel land, and all Longarm had to do was figure a way to separate Gettis from his army of toughs and bring him back to the army in chains.

The nearest army post was outside the town of Banning, a good hard two days' ride, and Longarm had about as good a chance of capturing Gettis and taking him that distance as he had of hazing a longhorn bull through the eye of a needle. Still, he had no call to throw in the towel. Not yet, anyway. He would just have to wait and see what cards fate dealt him in this deal, then play his hand as best he could.

Chapter 6

After a short nap, Longarm went downstairs to see if he
could maybe have a chat with Carlotta. She wasn't in
the kitchen, but when he glanced out the kitchen window he saw her outside in the fenced-in yard alongside
the boardinghouse, doing the washing in a huge wooden
tub. Ventura, her sleeves rolled up past her elbows, was
using a large washboard to scrub the sheets clean and
Carlotta was busy hauling hot water.

He left the kitchen and descended the side porch
steps and started toward them. Brushing aside a lock of
damp hair plastered to her forehead, Carlotta turned to
face Longarm as he neared her.

"I am busy, Custis," she told him.

"I can see that."

She smiled wanly. "This have to be done. Clean bed-
sheets do not come easy."

"I can appreciate that," he said. "Why not take a break and join me in the kitchen for a cup of coffee?"

She hesitated only a minute; then, with a barely perceptible sigh, she turned, said something to Ventura, and proceeded ahead of Longarm into the kitchen. As she put on the coffeepot, Longarm slumped at the table and leaned back, his eyes on Carlotta.

Waiting for the coffee to heat up, Carlotta turned to look at him and met his gaze without wavering. "You still work for Jim Gettis?"

"Yes, but not as a bouncer."

"Oh?"

"I don't know what Gettis has in mind, but he says he wants me around. He trusts me."

"If that man trust you, I wonder about you, Custis."

"Sorry to hear you say that, Carlotta."

She brought the steaming coffeepot over to the table, filled his cup and hers, returned the pot to the stove, then joined him. She spooned sugar into her coffee without a word, obviously troubled. She had enjoyed Longarm as much as he had enjoyed her, and she was probably wondering if she had made a mistake. He didn't want her to think so.

"What is it, Carlotta? Why are you freezing up on me?"

"You do not know?"

"You don't like me working for Gettis."

She shrugged. "That is true. I am sorry I let you use my name."

"You hoped Gettis wouldn't give me a job."

She smiled at him, a little sadly. "Si. I did not think he would. And now you are his pet."

He winced internally at her characterization of him.

74

"There's more to this than your dislike of Gettis. What is it, Carlotta?"

She frowned. He could see she was wondering if she could trust Longarm to keep what she told him to himself. Then, evidently deciding she could, she took a deep breath and said, "You are right, Custis. There is more than I tell you. Now I will speak of it. This man, Gettis, I see him shoot down my father when he and his army of gunslicks take our ranch. He is a devil, that one. Someday, maybe, I kill heem!"

Longarm had not expected this. But recalling what he had learned from MacDuff, he understood perfectly the circumstances surrounding the killing of Carlotta's father—and her grim, implacable hatred of the man. He could understand also why she had kept this part of her past a secret from him—and from anyone else in town, he realized. At the same time he had renewed appreciation for Jim Gettis's need for bodyguards, and why Carlotta was now running a boardinghouse in Copper City.

"Well, I guess there's nothing I can say, Carlotta. I understand why you hate the man. If I were in your shoes, I'd hate him, too."

"Why you need to be in my shoes, Custis? Is it not enough that I tell you what a monster thees dirty gringo is?"

"I need the job," Longarm protested, aware how lame that sounded.

"Then maybe you do not need to stay in my house!"

Longarm had expected that. With a gentle smile, he said, "You really mean you want me to go back to the Palace Hotel?"

"I think maybe you better," she said resolutely, her dark eyes cold and inflexible. "I will not give lodging any longer to a member of Jim Gettis's gang."

Longarm finished his coffee and stood up. Looking down at her, he said, "Maybe some day you'll see I'm not really a member of Jim Gettis's gang, Carlotta. Until then, adios."

"Adios," she said, her beautiful face sad.

Longarm left the kitchen and headed for the stairs, hoping wearily that this time he could get a room at the hotel with intact window shades. He was not optimistic.

Leaving the hotel an hour or so later, dressed in his vest and frock coat, Longarm was on his way down the street to Stella's for an early supper, when he caught sight of one of the housemen across the street in the act of stepping out into the traffic, his eyes on Longarm. He and the rest of his fellows must have learned by this time they were no longer employed. If so, Longarm could understand their unhappiness, and this man's apparent desire to discuss the matter with him.

Forced to step back out of the path of an ore wagon, the houseman kept his eyes focused on Longarm. This gent was the biggest of the four bouncers, a tough, sinewy individual with a well-oiled Colt strapped to his thigh. He was wearing a dark, wide-brimmed Stetson, its brim pulled down so that half his face was in shadow. Nevertheless his eyes were visible to Longarm, and they were as dark and menacing as the bores of two six-guns.

The ore wagon thundered on past, the freighter's whip snapping over the laboring horses, and the houseman continued on across the street to disappear into the mouth of an alley ahead of Longarm. Longarm could have crossed the street at this point and have avoided trouble, he supposed. But he saw no good reason to do this. If he didn't stand up to this fellow now in broad daylight, he'd likely get himself cut in two by a shotgun

76

blast while crossing in front of an alley some night. He unbuttoned his frock coat and kept going.

Fifteen paces from the alley entrance, he slowed. Those behind him were forced to skirt him and did so, making no effort to hide their irritation at his sudden slowing down. The houseman stepped out of the alley and confronted Longarm, his feet braced wide, the tail of his coat tucked behind the handle of his six-gun Longarm pulled up.

"You crybaby bastard," the ex-houseman said thickly, his face going beet red with suppressed indignation. He had obviously fortified himself with bravo juice, Longarm noted. "You got me fired."

"That's right. You and your fellows were too yellow to take me on by yourselves, so you hired them two miners. What makes you think you got the sand to take me on now?"

"Why, damn you . . ."

The man's right hand darted back, then halted, his fingers twitching over the grips of his revolver. Behind him Longarm saw pedestrians ducking for cover and he could hear others behind him scurrying out of the line of fire. Buggies and ore wagons pulled up hastily, their drivers leaping from their seats and heading for cover.

Longarm watched the man's eyes and saw his tongue snake out nervously. Tiny beads of sweat stood out on his face. He looked like he was straining to lay an egg.

Then the man blinked and his right hand dropped to his revolver.

Longarm reached across his belt and drew his .44, ducking low and crabbing out into the street as he did so. The houseman's draw was fast enough, and his six-gun was already jumping in his hand, but he was sending the two rounds at the spot where Longarm had been, not where he was. As he swung around to correct his aim, Longarm fired up at the man's chest, hoping for a heart shot. Instead, he caught the man high on the left shoulder.

The houseman was still game. He went down on one knee and brought up his six-gun. This time Longarm took his time and planted a slug between his eyes. The back of the houseman's head exploded in a pink cloud. Shards of bone and bloody patches of his brain appeared on the wall of the general store behind him. As the man collapsed back lifeless, his trigger finger pulsed reflexively on the trigger, and he sent three wild shots into the air past Longarm. A distant window somewhere behind him shattered.

Longarm stood up and walked over to gaze down at the foolish houseman. He was spread-eagled on his back, a dark, growing stain in the dust under his shattered skull. A helluva price to pay for losing a job, he thought grimly as he reloaded his six-gun and dropped it back into his cross-draw rig and buttoned up his frock coat.

By now the townsmen and miners had rushed to encircle him and the houseman, their eyes wild with excitement, some of the faces hanging open like those of a starved coyote circling a bear's kill. Abruptly, a man with a sheriff's badge pushed through them, and at the sight of Longarm pulled up warily, then went down on one knee beside the dead houseman. Finding no pulse in the man's wrist, he stood back up and faced Longarm.

"What happened here?" he demanded.

"He braced me when I reached the alley," Longarm told him.

The sheriff looked around at the crowd. "That right?" he demanded. "Anyone see this?"

A rough chorus of agreement came from all sides, corroborating Longarm's account. The sheriff looked back at Longarm.

"So he braced you. How come?"

"He didn't like getting fired, I guess. He was one of the Long Chance's bouncers, and Gettis got rid of him today. I guess he blamed me."

Frowning, the sheriff looked back down at the dead man. "Yeah. I heard about that. Gettis fired all four." He looked back up at Longarm. "Okay. You got enough witnesses to say it was self-defense. But maybe from now on you better make sure your back is covered."

"Thanks for the advice, Sheriff."

Longarm moved past him and cut through the crowd, which parted quickly for him. Entering the alley that led behind the Long Chance, he moved along it until he reached the saloon, then stepped into the back corridor. Gettis's two bodyguards were leaning against the wall beside his office door, and when they saw him, the nearest one to Longarm straightened up.

"I heard shots just now," he said. "What happened?"

"I met one of the fired bouncers," Longarm told him, brushing past him. "Excuse me, Shorty," he said as he knocked on Gettis's door.

"You mean you had a shoot-out with one of them?"

"Which one?" asked the other eagerly, his eyes lighting.

"The tall one."

"Sid Buckmaster?" He seemed astonished.

Before Longarm could reply, Jim Gettis pulled the door open. "What's going on out here?" he demanded.

Then he saw Longarm. "Was that you just knocked, Long?"

"It was."

"What do you want?"

"I figure we better talk."

"Oh? What about?"

"I just had to shoot Sid Buckmaster."

"You what—?"

"You heard me, Jim."

Gettis stepped back and pulled the door open wider. "Get in here," he said. As Longarm stepped past him into the room, Gettis poked his head back out into the corridor. "Shorty," he barked, "go find out what's going on."

Closing the door, Gettis indicated the chair by his desk with a nod. "Sit and rest your weary gun hand," he suggested, his eyes alight as he studied Longarm eagerly. "Let's have it."

Longarm placed his hat down on the corner of Gettis's desk and gave his account of the gunfight. When he finished, Gettis leaned back in his swivel chair and shook his head admiringly. "I knew you were the man I've been looking for." Then he leaned forward. "You hear about the run-in I had with the sheriff?"

"Nope."

"I threw Kincaid out of here not long after you left this morning. He landed so hard he broke the hitch rail out front. He's threatening to set up a rival saloon. He's getting too big for his britches, that one."

"What do you plan to do about him?"

"I wasn't sure. I am now. This business of yours with Sid Buckmaster has helped me make up my mind." Gettis got up from his chair and plucked his hat off a wall hook. "There's a bottle in the desk, Custis. Help yourself while I go round up some citizens."

He explained no further and left Longarm with the whiskey. Longarm had no more than a couple of fingers and was on his second cheroot when Gettis returned with three townsmen. They looked out of breath and were as confused about what Gettis had in mind as Longarm. But it was clear they were ready and willing to do his bidding.

After all, Copper City was his town.

The introductions were swift and Longarm made no real effort to keep the three townsmen's names clear in his mind, content to shake each hand that was thrust at him, then sit back and let Gettis make whatever move he had in mind.

"These here are the town's councilmen," Gettis told him. "The mayor ain't here. He's off somewhere, but we don't need him. He'd be outvoted anyway."

"Outvoted, Jim?" one of the councilmen asked.

He was a storekeeper, obviously, wearing a starched white shirt with red sleeve garters. His face was thin, his complexion sallow. A pair of spectacles were perched on his nose, and the smell of grain and freshly milled flour clung to him.

"That's right, Bill. Custis Long here is goin' to be our new town marshal."

The councilman standing beside Bill said, "But you said we didn't need one with Sheriff Kincaid so handy."

"He ain't handy no more. He's too busy with his girls," Gettis snapped. "So I say we give Long here a badge and let him use that empty office in back of your store, Bill."

"Well, sure, Jim, if you think that's best," Bill said, blinking owlishly through his silver-rimmed spectacles at Longarm.

"That's it, then," said Gettis. "By a vote of the town council, we got ourselves a town marshal. You can go back to your stores now, boys. Thanks for your time."

The three seemed used to such quick dismissals, and turning about, filed from Gettis's office without further debate. As soon as they were gone, Gettis strode around behind his desk and slumped heavily down in his chair, grinning at Longarm. He obviously enjoyed having a town of his own to run. It made things pretty damn convenient.

"Who's goin' to swear me in?" Longarm asked.

Reaching into a drawer, Gettis produced a tin star and flipped it across the desk at Longarm. "Pin that on," he said, "and consider yourself sworn in."

Longarm pinned the badge onto his vest.

"Now, then, let's get a few things straight," Gettis began, his face suddenly sober. "Kincaid ain't going to stand still for this, and the first thing we got to make clear to him is your jurisdiction."

"Which is?"

"Everything within the townsite. Kincaid has everything outside. This will give you all the legal authority you'll need to stop Kincaid from building any saloon for his girls in town. If we need new laws on that, the city council will draft them."

"And I'll be the lightning rod for any trouble Kincaid makes on this score."

"For which you will be paid handsomely. Two hundred a month and all your meals at Stella's."

"I might get sick of eatin' there."

"If you do, let me know. I'll have her cook fired."

Longarm laughed. The man's arrogance was unbounded, he realized. He stood up. "I'd like to go see my new office," he said, reaching for his hat.

"Sure. Go ahead. It's behind Bill Thompson's Feed and Grain Store on the corner, off the alley and just a few feet from the street. I'll see to it that you have a desk and chairs, and someone will put up a sign on the corner of the alley announcing your presence."

"If I have to jail anyone—for disturbing the peace, that sort of thing—where will I put them up?"

"There's a long room back of your office. I'll have it turned into a lockup. I'll send for window bars. For cells we'll just use regular wooden doors and straw mattresses for the drunks to sleep it off on. But you won't be doin' much of that, Long. That ain't why you're the town marshal."

"So you want me to go easy on the miners."

"Sure. Let my boys handle them. You just keep your ass down until Kincaid makes his move."

Longarm clapped his hat on. "See you, Jim."

As Longarm pulled open the door, Gettis called to him. Longarm paused and looked back. Gettis was grinning.

"Congratulations," he said.

The storekeeper showed Longarm his office. A much-used rolltop desk sat in one corner, a thin patina of flour dust over it. The swivel chair pushed up under it looked dangerous. Longarm reached over and rattled it. It was indeed unsteady.

"I'll have a new one brought in," Bill said hastily. "I didn't know anything about this until a half hour ago."

"I know," said Longarm. "I was there. Remember? That was the first I heard of it, too."

A leather-covered sofa rested along one wall. It had a few rips in it, and the stuffing was leaking out, but it looked comfortable enough. It too was covered with a fine film of flour dust. A calendar two years old had been nailed to the wall beside the desk, the two windows were grimy, and the floorboards squeaked.

But it would do well enough.

"Gettis said something about putting holding cells in the storeroom. Want to show it to me?"

"Sure," Bill said, absorbing this unexpected information without a murmur.

He stepped ahead of Longarm through a doorway into the adjoining storeroom. Following after him, Longarm saw that it would certainly be large enough once the barrels of flour and sacks of grain and other stock were moved out. The cells could be built along the back wall, each one with its own window. Not that Longarm intended to be here long enough to see any of this.

"Thanks, Bill," Longarm said. "I'd like it if you could see about that chair and get someone down here to get rid of the flour dust. Otherwise, I'll have a coughing fit and blow the whole place up."

"Sure thing, Mr. Long."

A moment later, pausing at the head of the alley, Longarm was about to head for Stella's when he heard his name called. Softly but urgently. He turned his head and saw Carlotta hurrying along the sidewalk toward him. He would not have recognized her if she hadn't called out to him. She was wearing a long, black, fringed dress and had tied a black kerchief over her head. He held up and waited for her to reach him.

"This is a pleasant surprise, Carlotta."

"Can I speak to you? Someplace alone?"

"As a matter of fact, we are only a few feet from my office."

"Office?"

84

He flipped aside his frock coat's lapel so she could see the marshal's star gleaming on his vest. "I'm the new marshal."

Her astonishment gave way to sudden concern. "You are as long as you remain alive, Custis. Let us go to your office. I have this thing to tell you."

He led her back down the alley and into his office. Closing the door securely, he remained standing while she sat forward on the edge of the sofa. Then he moved over to the desk and sat down on the edge of it, not trusting the chair.

"I'm listening, Carlotta."

"I am sorry you move out, Custis," she said. "It was not kind of me to speak like that with you. Sometimes I get so mad at that dog of a gringo, I say foolish things."

"No harm done, Carlotta. It would take a lot more than that to make me ungrateful to you. Is that why you came?"

"No. MacDuff, he hear things. He tell me and so I come to warn you."

"About what?"

"I hear about the gunfight with Buckmaster. Everyone is happy. He was a bully, especially to my people."

"Glad you approve."

"No. I do not approve of killing. I do not like to see one man kill another. But sometimes it is necessary."

"Like when it comes time for you to kill Gettis."

She blushed. "I talk silly when I am hurt, Custis. Forgive me."

"I shouldn't have said that. Now, what's this about warning me?"

"Tonight, the other housemen are planning to kill you."

"Oh?"

"MacDuff, he say he cannot tell you where he hear this, and he is not sure how they will do this thing. But he think maybe they will come for you when you sleep tonight in your bed."

"The hotel?"

"Yes."

"Thanks, Carlotta. And thank MacDuff for me, too."

She got up then and walked toward him. Longarm slipped off the desk and found her pressing hard against him. Wrapping her arms around his neck, she pulled his head down and kissed him on the lips warmly, passionately. He responded in kind. At the end of the kiss, he pushed herself gently from him, slipped the black silk kerchief back up over her head, and tied it under her chin.

"Be careful," she said.

He opened the office door for her. She looked in both directions before stepping out into the alley and hurrying off. Longarm watched her go, then took a deep breath. It looked like he would get very little sleep this night. He closed the office door and hurried up the alley, anxious to reach Stella's.

He was as hungry as a bear and would need nourishment if there was any truth at all in Carlotta's warning.

Chapter 7

Longarm sat in the corner of his room dozing, his .44 in his right hand, his rifle leaning against the wall beside him. A shadow loomed in the open window, followed by the sound of a boot glancing lightly off the outside window frame. Longarm's head shot up and he saw the man standing on the hotel's back-porch roof, his two hands closed about the window sash as he slowly pushed it higher.

Longarm focused his eyes on the boot cautiously stepping through the window. When it came to rest on the floor beneath it, a head followed after it, kept low to clear the window sash, and then the man was inside the room, standing in front of the window, staring over at the bed where Longarm had fashioned a reasonable dummy of blankets and pillows.

Longarm recognized the bouncer from his mustache

and the thick, unruly strands of hair sticking out from under his hat brim. If the man had paused a moment to look behind him, he would have found himself staring into the bore of Longarm's .44 less than four feet away. Instead, he took a cautious step toward the bed, his own Colt out and extended, the barrel gleaming dully in the moonlight slanting in through the window.

Longarm kept as quiet as he could, wondering where the others were. Carlotta had said *they* were coming after him, meaning more than one—three to be exact. The door opened, the latch clicking softly as it slipped free. In a moment the second houseman stole silently into Longarm's hotel room. This one too had his six-gun out and was pointing it at the bed.

One more to go, Longarm thought. The third man. Maybe this one would step out of the closet.

He was about to give up on him when the third man's shadow blocked out the moonlit window From where he stood, he could not see Longarm hunched up against the wall. This one made no attempt to climb into the room, however—content to watch from the roof and add his two cents only if circumstances warranted. A shrewd move. And one that made things a mite more difficult for Longarm.

Longarm waited. He had long since decided that he would wait for his would-be assailants to make the first move. The man who came in the window thumb-cocked, leveled his gun—and fired. At the same time his companion also cut loose. Longarm saw the cotton blanket leaping as the slugs slammed through them. Feathers from the two pillows leaped up from the bed. The walls seemed to pulse with each detonation, and white coils of smoke drifted toward the low ceiling, the smell of cordite suddenly strong in the small room.

The two men paused. The detonations ceased. Smoking gun in hand, the first houseman to enter approached the bed, Longarm waited no longer. Aiming for the man's spine inches above his rectum, Longarm sent one round, then a second into him, the force of the slugs catapulting him forward onto the bed. The man beside him turned. Longarm sent two rounds into him, aiming low, for his crotch.

The window shattered as the one on the roof fired through at Longarm. The slug slammed into the wall above him, showering him with plaster. Longarm lunged across the room and ducked behind the bed. The man on the roof fired another round at him. The slug plowed into the mattress, causing a sudden puff of smoke as it ignited the ticking. Longarm came up behind the bed and fired his last round through the window at the dark figure crouching on the roof. He heard the man cry out, then saw him dart away from the window. Longarm leaped over the bed, snatched up his rifle, and crashed through the window, sending shards of glass and window sash flying. He hit the roof running and saw the houseman clambering off the roof.

Longarm darted over and peered over the edge. The man was shimmying down a rope and had almost reached the ground. He looked up. When he saw Longarm peering down at him, he panicked, let go of the rope and dropped clumsily to the ground and started to limp over to the three waiting horses. Tucking the rifle's stock into his shoulder, Longarm tracked him carefully, then held up. It would be like shooting a fish in a barrel. He had already accounted for two of them.

Longarm lowered his rifle and watched the frantic houseman gallop off down the alley. Then he turned and climbed back through the shattered window.

● ● ●

"A one-man army, that's what you are," said Gettis, shaking his head for the third time.

"I didn't see as I had any choice in the matter," Longarm explained, leaning back in Gettis's chair. "They were out to get me. It was kill or be killed."

"Well, the bastard that got away is Tim Horner. He'll be comin' back at you. You were a fool not to take him out when you could."

"Maybe so."

"I think Custis did just fine," Casey said, "It's just a lucky thing he was such a light sleeper."

It was early the next morning, and Casey had entered the saloon with Gettis, as eager as he was, it seemed, to get the full story of last night's shoot-out. She was sitting up on the corner of the desk and looked sensational in a bottle-green dress she must have had to pour herself into. Tipped back on her head was a white, broad-brimmed sun hat, her golden curls spilling down onto her shoulders.

"One thing's for sure," Gettis said. "After this, I can't see that there'll be many drunks sassin' you, and sure as hell Kincaid won't bother you after this. That demonstration last night was as good as a showdown. I'm glad you're on my team, Custis."

"Does that mean I get a raise?"

"I'm not *that* glad," Gettis said, laughing.

Longarm got to his feet. "They've given me another room at the hotel. I think I'll get some sleep."

"How *can* you in this heat?" Casey asked.

"I haven't slept much since midnight. I'm bone weary. I'll sleep."

"Go ahead, Marshal," Gettis said. "Get some shut-eye. You deserve it. I'll see you when you start your rounds, if I'm still in town."

Longarm clapped on his hat, touching the brim in polite deference to Casey, then left the office and stepped out through the back door into the alley, heading for the hotel. He hadn't lied. He was exhausted—so much so he felt unsteady on his feet, almost as if he were drunk.

But now, thanks to Carlotta's timely warning, he could sleep. He had been careful not to tell Gettis of the warning provided by MacDuff and relayed to him by Carlotta. He felt it was best to do all he could to keep those two out of it. He wasn't sure why, exactly. It was just a feeling he had.

He entered the hotel the back way, mounted the steps to his room, and pushed into it. Slamming the door shut behind him, he collapsed facedown on the bed and kicked off his boots. He was asleep before the bedsprings stopped rocking under him.

It was still daylight when a light but insistent rap on the door awakened him. He stirred, blinked at the late, slanting beams of light streaming across the room, heard the rapping come again, and sat up on the bed.

"Who is it?" he called.

There was no answer, just another urgent rapping.

Cautiously, he padded across the room and opened the door and was astonished to see Casey standing in the hallway. She slipped quickly into the room and pushed the door shut behind her. Then she swept off her sun hat and shook out her curls.

"What is it, Casey?" Longarm asked. "Trouble?"

"If you mean does Jim want you, the answer is no. It's me that wants to talk, Custis."

91

Longarm was not yet fully awake, the tendrils of sleep still clouding his brain. His mouth was dry also. Sleeping in the daytime was not usual for him. "I got some rye on the dresser," he told Casey, scratching his head and blinking his eyes to get the sand out. "I think I'll need some to wake me up."

"If you've got two glasses, I'll join you."

"I've only got one glass, but I can use the bottle and you can have the glass."

"You are a real gentleman."

"And you are a real lady."

Casey was still wearing the bottle green dress, and still looked sensational, and, despite the heat, as cool as a tall glass of lemonade. He unstoppered the bottle, poured a couple of fingers into his glass and handed it to her. She lifted it in a toast.

"Cheers."

He touched her glass with the bottle, then lifted it to his lips and took a healthy belt as she downed the two fingers, swallowing the rye as easily as she would a glass of spring water. Casey then walked over and made herself comfortable in the small easy chair beside the window. Longarm sat down on the edge of the bed, facing her.

"Well, now, Casey," Longarm said, "what brings you into the spider's parlor, if it is not Jim Gettis?"

"It is not. This may surprise you, Custis, but I come and go as I please."

Longarm smiled and, leaning forward, poured two more fingers into her glass. "Of course it surprises me. I've heard what a tight rein he keeps on you."

She sighed and looked glumly at her glass. "You're right. He does, at that. But don't worry, Custis. I came up the back stairs."

"A wise precaution. Now, are you going to tell me what this is all about?"

"I'm curious."

"Curious?"

"Yes. About you."

"You think I'm up to something?"

"All I know is I have this feeling about you."

"Woman's intuition."

"It's more than that."

"Go on."

"I don't think you are what you're pretending to be."

"And just what am I pretending to be, Casey?"

"A drifter. Someone willing to do any man's bidding if the pay is right. There's more to you than that. A lot more."

"Maybe you're seeing more than what's in front of you, Casey. Quite a few make that mistake, you know."

She laughed shortly, bitterly. "I've made that mistake myself more than once."

"So why not accept me on face value, Casey. Let sleeping dogs lie."

"Are you a sleeping dog, Custis?"

He paused a moment, studying her carefully. "What are you after, Casey?"

"I told you. I came up here because I wanted to know more about you. In a way, you're too good to be true."

"Casey, don't you like what you've got here? An alliance with a strong man like Gettis? I understand he's built you a fine home in Copper City, a two-story mansion shaded with cottonwoods. And in back a fountain with a real grass lawn around it. Not bad for this country."

"I have everything a woman could want, Custis. Except one thing."

"And what might that be."

"Freedom."

"You're just a bird in a gilded cage."

"Yes."

"What's to stop you from packing up and taking the next stage out?"

"Jim. He'd come after me and bring me back. And if I wouldn't come quietly and submissively, he'd kill me."

"You must be exaggerating."

"You don't know Jim Gettis the way I do. He's insanely jealous. He told me once that if he couldn't have me, no one else could."

"You shouldn't believe crazy talk like that."

"Shouldn't I? Two years ago, I packed a picnic basket, rented a buggy from the livery, and rode out of town to find a stream. I wanted to bathe in fresh water for a change. Something I used to love to do when I was a kid."

She paused to sip her drink before going on.

"I found a stream in among some cottonwoods, undressed, and had my bath. I was still in the water when one of Jim's Mexican punchers saw my horse and buggy and rode up to investigate. He was as embarrassed as I was when he found out it was me, and backed off. After I dressed, he dismounted to apologize. That was when Jim rode up. I could tell right away what Jim was thinking, but before I could say anything, he hit me so hard I went down and was out of it for almost five minutes. When I woke up, the Mexican was hanging from a limb."

Longarm was impressed. "I see."

"Jim told me afterward that if he ever caught me with another man, he'd kill both of us."

"And you believe him."

"Of course I believe him. Do you blame me?"

"No, I guess not." He took a swig from the bottle. "But what do you want me to do about it, Casey?"

"I want you to tell me if my hunch is right."

"Your hunch?"

"That you came here to find Gettis. That you're after him."

"Jesus. What on earth would make you think that?"

"I know Jim's got a past. A bad one. That's the only explanation I can see for those bodyguards that follow him everywhere."

"And you think I might be a lawman or something— come to this godforsaken place to bring him to justice?"

She shrugged, the hope in her eyes fading. "I know it sounds silly."

"Silly! Downright crazy."

She finished her drink. "You can't blame a woman for hoping."

"What you're suggesting, Casey, is that if I were a lawman, you would turn on Gettis and help me bring him in."

"You make it sound so—underhanded."

"Well, isn't it?"

"I suppose it is," she said wearily, getting to her feet. "It was foolish of me to suggest such a thing. It's just so hard for me to believe you're for real, Long. If you know what I mean."

"No, I don't."

"Well, the thing is, you don't *look* like a gunslick or a drifter. And you don't talk like one, either."

"I'm sorry to disappoint you, Casey."

"Damn it, Long. You know what I mean."

Lonagrm shrugged. "All right, Casey. Let's just for-

95

get we had this conversation. No harm done, and I'm glad for the visit."

She smiled, getting to her feet. "You're a real gentleman, Long."

Longarm placed the bottle of rye down on top of the dresser and stood up. He intended to walk across the room to open the door for Casey. But before he could start for it, she stepped into his path, then thrust herself boldly, provocatively against him. What the hell, Longarm thought as he pulled her closer. Sure, it was crazy. This was no way to put himself in good with his new boss. But a wild recklessness always lurking just below the surface took hold of him—that, and the heady perfume exuded by this ripe, experienced woman.

She flung her arms around his neck and leaned back, grinding her pelvis against his crotch with a lovely, wanton lasciviousness, chuckling deeply all the while. They kissed. After the kiss, they spun, still in each other's arms, and landed on the bed. He yanked up her skirt and placed his hand on her leg, then moved it swiftly up her thigh. Reaching her crotch, he felt her moist, silken pubis and found she had come prepared. There was nothing under Casey's dress but Casey.

Laughing, she flung her dress aside and spread her legs wide to accept him. Peeling out of his long johns, Longarm flung himself astride her and plunged home. She gasped and hauled up her legs, scissoring his waist, sucking him deep into her. She was soft and warm and wet, and he plunged home, all the way, the feel of her cervix hard against his tip. He lunged repeatedly, his head back, riding her hell-bent for glory—until at last he came in one wild, marvelous spasm that set her off in turn, causing her to explode under him like a string of Chinese firecrackers.

Still inside her, panting heavily, he collapsed face-down onto her incandescent breasts, utterly spent—and felt her unquenched heat flow deep into him. She put her arms about his neck and pressed his face deeper into her expansive cleft. Turning his head, he let his lips close about a nipple. He pulled on it teasingly. She laughed and ran her fingers through his hair. To his astonishment his erection came alive once again, acquiring a life of its own as it quickened and began to probe deeper into her warmth, as insatiable as the woman under him. Casey cried out in delight as she felt his erection growing eagerly within her. Then, laughing softly—the laughter coming from deep within her—she hugged him still closer to her ample breasts.

"You ain't still suspicious of me, are you?" he asked, working himself still deeper, probing for her bottom.

"If I am, it sure don't matter," she sighed, moving lasciviously under him. "Sure, I was wondering about you and why a man with your talents would be willing to work for an animal like Jim Gettis. But I was also wondering about something else."

"And what might that be?"

"If you could maybe satisfy a woman as well as you could fight. Seeing you in action, Long, got me a mite worked up. I am afraid it made me . . . lust after you."

"You are a shameless woman."

"I know, but I can't help myself."

"How are you going to explain this long absence, Casey?"

"Jim's out to his ranch. He'll be gone all afternoon. Besides, it's too late to be thinking of that now." She hugged him closer, her eyes burning with a reckless fire. "I've waited too long for a good man—someone like you—to come along, and I ain't waitin' no longer."

97

"Jim Gettis doesn't strike me as less than a man. Far from it."

"He's a pig," she said with sudden, snarling bitterness. "He grunts like a pig and smells like a pig. I might as well be a barn animal for all the difference it makes to him. He doesn't make love, he defecates into me, then utters some foul obscenity and backs off, hauling up his britches. He doesn't even take off his boots, for Christ's sake!"

"Doesn't sound so good, at that."

"My God, Custis, I'm a woman who loves to love. Always have, but that man would turn the mother of all whores into a nun."

"Enough said," Longarm told her. "Never like to hear a woman bitch about another man when I'm beddin' her."

"Fair enough."

She sighed then and spread her thighs luxuriously, easing up under him until he could feel his scalding tip nudging against the depths of her sex.

"Mmmm," she murmured, "Oh, Long. That's lovely! Keep going now. Don't stop. Please!"

"Got no intention of stopping," he grunted as he leaned deep into her.

He had been with ample, well-endowed women before. But Casey was a revelation. Despite her lush ripeness, she was not heavy at all, but light and supple—her breasts enough and more than enough to satisfy any man. She was pure, undiluted delight. That Jim Gettis would kill to keep her in his corral was perfectly understandable. That he would not have sense enough to make the most of it was not.

He increased his pace, his knees digging into the bed.

"Yes, yes!" she cried eagelry. "Keep going! Don't stop now!"

He didn't bother to reply as he pounded into her. She hugged him closer fiercely until he felt as if she were surrounding him completely, shutting out everything but the awesome, fiery glow of her body.

Unwilling to hold back, his pace increased. She laughed throatily and lifted her knees, enabling him to plow still deeper, opening up and swallowing his erection effortlessly, then tightening her inner muscles about it with the strength of a closed fist. He pounded deeper and still deeper into her. She rocked back, lifting him higher. He plunged down onto her and found she needed no cushions under her buttocks.

Approaching his climax, he tried to hold back, but she would have none of it, grabbing him to her with a wild, unthinking ferocity. There was no need to wait, he realized, and he came, ejaculating deep into her. With a soft, feral howl she climaxed herself in sudden, quickening spasms, mewling like a mountain cat, her eyes rolling back in her head, sucking his juices deep into her and milking his erection repeatedly until at last a deep satisfied groan escaped her lips and she released him to lie still under him, her eyes closed, her breathing coming in short, sharp gasps.

He eased off her, rested his cheek on his palm and let his eyes follow her lovely curves and valleys, the lift of her full, upthrust breasts, the rise of her belly, followed by the dark, moist gleam of her pubic patch. A fine patina of perspiration covered her from head to toe. The frantic exertion of a moment before had dampened her hair, causing it to curl; golden tendrils coiled about her nipples. She was all woman. That was for damn sure. But she was trouble, too, the kind of trouble he never seemed able to avoid—or wanted to avoid.

She opened her eyes and smiled up ath im, then blew out her cheeks. "That should keep me," she told him. "For a while, anyway."

"Me, too."

"It's so nice to be with a real man—one who doesn't roll over and start snoring."

"You're a lot of woman, Casey."

"As good as Carlotta?"

Longarm was surprised—and annoyed—but he did not allow himself to show it. "What about her, Casey?"

"She's a woman and you're a man. If she gave you a bath in that back room of hers, she gave you something else as well—later. I know her."

"I told you, Casey. I don't like to hear about other men—or other women—when I'm with someone."

She sighed and sat up. "I'm sorry. I'm a bitch sometimes. I admit it. I should cut my tongue out I suppose, but that would be too painful. Forgive me?"

"There's nothing to forgive," Longarm said, reaching for his long johns.

With an audible sigh, Casey leaned off the bed and caught hold of her dress and pulled it up onto the bed beside her. Conversation done. Time for life to get back on the track.

They dressed in silence. He let her out after checking the hallway outside his door, then stood by the door to listen as her footfalls faded on the back steps. Then he took a deep breath and walked back to his bed. He didn't move too fast, not after what he had just been through. Casey had hauled his ashes so completely he felt as light as a feather. He had the giddy conviction that any sudden movement might cause him to rise off the floor and slam into the wall.

This had been a pleasant enough interlude, all right. More than that, a lesson in unfettered lust and wild, peeled-back passion. But there was something more behind this afternoon's tryst, as well. In more ways than one, Longarm had been seduced, and what he wondered now was what further seductions Casey had in mind.

Chapter 8

A day later Longarm was sweeping out his office, wondering as he did how long he was going to have to keep up this masquerade, when a shadow filled his open doorway. He looked up to see MacDuff stepping into his office. With some relief Longarm leaned his broom in a corner. As he did so, he winced at the sudden crescendo of hammering that erupted from the adjacent storehouse.

"What's going on in there?" MacDuff asked, wincing along with Longarm.

"They're building cells for my prisoners," Longarm replied laconically.

"Can we go somewhere?"

"Sure," Longarm said. "It's early yet. The town's quiet. They got a fresh stock of Maryland rye in the hotel bar."

"Lead the way," said MacDuff, smiling quickly.

They found a quiet booth in the back of the hotel's saloon. Longarm poured the rye for both of them. "Thanks, MacDuff," Longarm said, "for that information you passed on to Carlotta. It probably saved my life."

MacDuff nodded, threw the rye down his throat, and shoved the glass forward for a refill. Longarm obliged promptly. MacDuff nodded his thanks and pulled the glass to him. "One of them got away, I hear."

"He did, but I think he lost his enthusiasm for back-shooting."

"Maybe he did, maybe he didn't. I wouldn't cross in front of many dark alleys for a while if I were you."

"I'll keep that in mind, MacDuff." Longarm took out a couple of cheroots, handed one to MacDuff, then bit off the end of his and lit up, after which he held the match out and lit MacDuff's smoke. Leaning back, he said, "How's Carlotta?"

"Fine. Still runs the best boardinghouse in the southwest. How much did she tell you about herself, Long?"

"Not much—except that her father was killed by Jim Gettis."

MacDuff nodded grimly. "That's only part of it. Did she tell you that for a while she rode with a small band of Mexicans who did all they could to wipe out Gettis?"

"No, she didn't."

"She wouldn't admit it, of course. But I can't help feeling that one of the reasons she's in town here running this boardinghouse is to get closer to Gettis."

"And kill him?"

"I know it sounds crazy."

"She hates him enough. I know that much." Longarm studied the editor. "Is this the reason for your visit to my office?"

"Nope. That just occurred to me now when you asked about Carlotta. What I came to tell you was that our deputy sheriff has got his back up, and you'd better watch out."

"Why?"

"Because he sees you standing between him and Gettis."

"You mean Kincaid's getting ready to make a move?"

"No doubt of it. And soon. Especially after the way Gettis humiliated him in front of the town. I hear his girls've been giving him plenty of lip since it happened. But he won't go after Gettis alone."

"He's got help?"

MacDuff nodded as he gulped down the rest of his rye and pushed the empty glass toward Longarm. Longarm filled the editor's glass to the brim and watched as the man drew it carefully toward him, in a sweat lest he spill a drop. "His help rode in with him this morning. Two Mexicans. Juan Taurez and Hipachi Leon. Carlotta knows them both. They're the reason she left that Mexican band."

"Carlotta sent you then."

MacDuff grinned. "That's right. This time you're in *her* debt. You made a hit with her, looks like."

Longarm shook his head in wonder. "I know, but it doesn't make much sense—not with me working for Jim Gettis, the man who killed her father."

"Women are crazy," MacDuff said, "God bless 'em."

"So they are. You realize, of course, I'll have to warn Gettis."

MacDuff shrugged. "Carlotta realized that, too. But,

hell, Gettis must know already that Kincaid is steaming. And everyone in town saw him ride in with them two Mexicans. My guess is Carlotta's hopin' you'll cut loose of Gettis now and let him sink or swim without you getting involved."

"I wish I could do that."

"Why can't you?"

"I can't go into that now, MacDuff."

MacDuff pushed his empty glass at Longarm, who promptly filled it. Savoring the rye, MacDuff cocked his head and studied Longarm for a long minute. "I'm trying to figure you out," he said. "But I'm damned if I can. You ain't what you seem. Carlotta told me this and I think she's right. But there's nothing I can put a finger on. Just Carlotta's word."

"A woman's intuition."

"It's more than that with Carlotta." He chuckled. "I suppose a woman feels she knows a man if she's slept with him."

"Watch it, MacDuff."

MacDuff waved his hand, as if to dismiss out of hand his indiscretion. "Meant nothing by it, Long. Nothin' at all. She's a fine, healthy woman. I envy you her regard."

Longarm pulled the bottle closer, stoppered it, and got up. "Thank Carlotta for me."

MacDuff finished what was left in his glass, then blinked foggily up at Longarm. "Quite all right, Long. Quite all right. Any time."

The editor should not have drunk so much rye on an empty stomach, Longarm noted to himself. But it was not his concern. It was Longarm's belief that every man has a right to decide for himself on such matters.

Taking the bottle with him, Longarm nodded curtly to MacDuff, turned on his heel, and left the hotel to return to his office.

He was checking on the construction of the new cells, requesting that the carpenters hurry things up, when he became aware of someone entering the marshal's office. He returned to it and found he had three visitors: Deputy Sheriff Bull Kincaid and his two Mexican gunslicks. As he closed the door behind him and crossed over to his desk, he nodded curtly to the three, mentally grateful to MacDuff and Carlotta for the warning they had provided.

Not that it was about to give him much of an advantage.

"What do you want, Kincaid?" Longarm asked the deputy sheriff, slumping into his chair.

"An understanding."

"That so?"

The big, round-faced man pulled out a polka-dot handkerchief and wiped off the sweat that ribboned the dirt on his heavy face. "That's so," he said angrily, his tone heavily belligerent.

Longarm could see that Bull Kincaid was an angry man and that the stove-top heat in this town was not doing anything for his temper. It was clear that the deputy sheriff's humiliation at the hands of Jim Gettis had seared itself into Bull Kincaid's soul, turning him into an unreasonable, angry man. And a dangerous one, to boot.

His two Mexican sidekicks attested to that.

They wore dark leather leggings, dark shirts, and ragged ponchos of dark green. Longarm caught the outline of crossed cartridge belts under the ponchos, and strapped to their thighs were gleaming side arms, the cleanest thing about them. On their heads sat black sombreros, their huge brims shadowing their faces. Out of the shadows their eyes gleamed coldly, malevolently at Longarm. They were in the land of the hated gringo and were making no effort to hide their implacable hatred.

One of them was short in stature, but powerfully built with a swarthy, pock-marked face. The other was taller, leaner, with gaunt, hollow cheeks and a drooping handlebar mustache. He was obviously consumptive and looked like Death on horseback, which probably made him more dangerous than the average *bandido*. Better to die with a bullet in his brain, he probably figured, than by strangling on his own bloody sputum.

Looking them over, Longarm found it difficult to believe that Carlotta had rode with men of this stripe. Maybe MacDuff had exaggerated.

"You going to introduce your friends, Kincaid?"

"These here are my two deputies."

"And I'll bet you swore them in yourself. Wait'll the sheriff in Travis hears about these two. How'd you find them? Turn over rocks in a damp place?"

The pock-marked Mexican took a step forward, his hand dropping to the butt of his Colt. Longarm leaned back and laughed in his face, then hauled his feet up onto his desk, allowing his frock coat to fall open to reveal his cross-draw rig. The smile on his face remained, but his eyes went cold as he waited for the foolish Mexican to slap leather.

"Go ahead, bandido," Longarm told him easily. "Make your move."

"No, for Christ's sake, Juan!" Kincaid cried, pulling the Mexican back. "Not now! Not here!"

Longarm grinned sardonically back at the agitated, profusely sweating deputy sheriff. "That's right, Kincaid. Not now. Wait until it gets dark. Is that the understanding you want with me?"

"Damn it, Long. This ain't personal, but you know and I know why Gettis set you up as the town marshal. To stop me. To squeeze me out, make me a laughingstock. You deny that?"

"Nope. And from where I sit, that's a shrewd move on his part."

"Maybe so. And maybe you think you can stop me. But now I want that bastard, and all I want from you is your word you won't interfere."

"If I go along, what's in it for me?"

"For you?"

"Sure. You think I'd step aside and give you a clean shot at Gettis without a deal of some kind?"

Kincaid swallowed. "How much you want?"

"Half of what you'll get when you take over. Half of every whore house, every gambling hall."

"I wasn't thinking of letting you in—or anyone else."

"Then why in hell should I make it easy for you to take out Gettis?"

Kincaid glanced at his two bandidos. "I just figured you wouldn't want to tangle with my two friends here. What the hell. Ain't it worth something if we let you ride out of here in one piece?"

"I see. If I go along, you'll let me live."

"That's the deal," said Kincaid, his eyes mean.

"And do I have your word on this?"

"Sure. You got my word."

Longarm smiled broadly. "And of course I trust you. After all, how could I doubt the word of a man who

runs a string of whores? Why would a man like you—
hard-working, law-abiding, a deputy sheriff and all—
go back on his word."

Not exactly sure of Longarm's drift, Kincaid frowned
uneasily. "You makin' fun of me?"

"I don't have to, Kincaid. You can do that all by
yourself."

"Damn your eyes! No more of this!" Kincaid cried
angrily, his face darkening with frustration. "What's
your answer? You goin' to step aside, or not?"

"Get out of here, Kincaid, and take these two sacks
of horseshit with you. Their stench is already curling the
woodwork."

Juan and Hipachi apparently understood English well
enough. At Longarm's words, they both took a step
closer to his desk. Longarm's smile broadened as he
reached calmly across his belt buckle, pulled out his
Colt, and laid it down on the desk in front of him, his
finger resting idly on the trigger. The Mexicans froze.

"You'll regret this, Long," Kincaid snarled. "I gave
you a chance to haul ass, but you blew it. You won't get
a second chance."

"Shove it up your ass, Kincaid."

The deputy sheriff hauled the two Mexicans around
and shoved them out of the office ahead of him. Longarm watched them go, pulled his feet down off his desk,
and got up. It was hot enough with the door open, but
for effect he strode to the door and slammed it shut
behind the departing delegation.

Then he dropped his Colt back into his holster and
slumped back down in his chair to do some hard thinking.

• • •

Nodding curtly to the bodyguard holding up the wall outside Gettis's door, Longarm knocked once, then pushed into the office. Gettis was standing before the desk with Calder, both men poring over a large map of the town open on the desk before them. They turned about on his entrance. Calder's cold, sunken eyes glittered with an excitement that made Longarm realize that they knew already what he had come to tell them.

"What's up, Long?" Gettis inquired, his shrewd eyes appraising Longarm closely. "You look like someone stepped on your tail."

"I just had some visitors."

"Visitors?"

"Kincaid and two hired gunmen."

Calder snorted. "You mean he brought them two greasers in to see you?"

Longarm nodded.

"And you weren't intimidated, I see."

"Maybe you should be. They didn't look like Sunday school parsons."

"No, they don't, and that's a fact. But we're way ahead of you," Gettis told Longarm. "The whole town's talking about them two greaseballs Kincaid brought in. I know them both. They ain't worth a fart in a windstorm."

"Kincaid wants me to step aside. He wants a clear shot at you."

"That's what I figured he was up to. You did right comin' to me. Proves you're loyal. I appreciate that, Long."

"Then you're not worried any?"

"Hell, no. This is just what I been hopin' for. I

pushed on him a little, and now he's playin' right into my hands. Ain't nothing going to get past my men. When Kincaid and them two greasers make their move, my boys will cut them down—and you'll be the only lawman left in town. Hell, as soon as it's over, I'm sending you to Travis so the county sheriff there can deputize you in Kincaid's place."

"You think he'd do that?"

"Why wouldn't he—when he hears what Kincaid's been up to around here."

Calder spoke up then, a grin on his lean, ravaged face. "Don't forget, Long. We'll have the goods on him, sure enough. Running a string of girls. Hiring Mexicans to murder an American citizen. Hell, we'll probably get a medal from that sheriff."

Longarm nodded. "If it goes the way you figure."

"Relax, Long. It will."

Longarm backed toward the door and opened it. "I'll be in my office if you need me."

Gettis nodded, then turned his attention back to the map of the city they had spread out on the top of the desk, effectively dismissing Longarm. Calder didn't bother to nod good-bye. The two of them were sure as hell taking this cool, Longarm noted, as he left the office and stepped out into the back alley and the afternoon's awful, searing heat.

It was close to midnight and Longarm was sitting on the front porch of Bill Thompson's Feed and Grain Store, his chair tipped back against the clapboards, his feet crossed on top of the railing. His hat was chucked back off his forehead and he had opened his shirt collar to let the chill night wind from the distant peaks cool his heat-drained body. It had turned out to be a surprisingly quiet night, and Longarm was enjoying his first cheroot of the night. His bottle of Maryland rye sat close by his chair.

Longarm had dutifully made his rounds throughout the evening. Due to his reputation, he had found not a single miner willing to tangle with him. Two hours earlier he had caught one grizzled old-timer in the act of carrying off one of Kincaid's girls. He was heading for his shack in the foothills. Longarm had come running in response to the girl's cries and when the miner saw him approaching, he had dumped the girl and run off. To Longarm's surprise, the girl had been upset with him for discouraging the miner, and after brushing herself off, had gone back to her crib in a huff. Her protests had, it seemed, been only for show. The prospect of a quiet night in the old miner's bed had apparently appealed to her.

Now, before going upstairs to the stifling heat of his hotel room, he was going over his options. As he saw it, his problem was to keep Jim Gettis alive so he could be brought in and hanged. But did that mean he should do all he could to keep the man from being taken out by Kincaid? After all, what would be the loss if Kincaid and his two Mexican sidekicks did manage to finish Gettis off? It would finally close the books on Gettis and Longarm could return forthwith to the cool, salubrious climate of the Mile High City.

Only this was not what the army wanted.

On the way from Fort Apache, Longarm's stagecoach had stopped overnight at Travis. Longarm had hired a buggy and ridden out to Fort Crook, a small border army post a few miles south of the town. There he had made himself known to the commanding officer, Major Paul Danton. The major had made it perfectly clear that what the army desperately wanted—and needed—was for Longarm to capture Gettis alive. An example had to be made. Desertions were increasing at an alarming rate in this impoverished peacetime army, especially here in this land of searing sun and grinding dust, and the army could not afford to lose this opportunity to show potential deserters just how long and persistent the army's reach could be—and how summary and final would be its punishment of those who attempted it.

Longarm and Major Danton discussed the situation in some detail and made what plans they could in the event that Longarm was able to apprehend Gettis. The difficulty, as the major had correctly pointed out, would be to separate Gettis from his bodyguards long enough for Longarm to transport him to the fort's stockade.

So far, Longarm's course of action—do everything to gain Gettis's confidence—had been working reasonably well. And with this accomplished, all that remained was for Longarm to separate Gettis from his bodyguards somehow and take him into custody so he could deliver him to Major Danton at Fort Crook. If Longarm could not manage this, he would have to find an excuse to ride alone to Fort Crook and arrange for an army detachment to be sent to Copper City. The sight of the army detachment riding into town would more than likely force Gettis into making a break for the border. It would be up to Longarm then to intercept the man before he crossed it—if he could do so.

But this was only conjecture, fruitless wool-gathering. For the moment, all Longarm could do was sit tight and play whatever cards fate dealt him. And hope that this fool Kincaid did not screw things up for him.

Longarm reached down, lifted the bottle of Maryland rye off the porch and set it down on his lap. Carefully unstoppering it, he raised the bottle to his lips and tipped his head back. A shot from the alley's mouth beside him disintegrated the bottle, sending a shower of rye and glass shards down his shirtfront. Longarm flung himself off the chair, drawing his .44 as he did so, then dove off the porch into the shadows beside the steps. A second shot from across the street slammed into the steps beside him.

Longarm lunged for the corner of the building. Son-of-a-bitch! He should have known this was coming! If Kincaid and his Mexican army couldn't get him out of town with threats, they'd get rid of him the old-fashioned way. They'd bushwhack him.

Rounding the corner of the feed and grain store, Longarm dashed into the alley beside it, seeking the protection of its shadows. He was almost to the end of it when he saw Bull Kincaid's silhouette step into view ahead of him. Longarm held up and flatttened himself against the wall. Kincaid heard him and ducked into the shadow of the hotel on the other side of the alley. His six-gun roared, the gunpowder lancing out of its muzzle. The bullet slammed into the wall beside Longarm. Longarm ducked low, then crabbed sideways, away from the wall, firing back at the point of the gun flash as he did so. His bullet slammed into a water barrel, and Longarm heard the rainwater pouring onto the floor of the alley with the impact of a horse pissing.

Kincaid's running figure materialized out of the darkness beside the barrel. Longarm snapped another shot at him a moment before Kincaid vanished around the corner of the hotel. Kincaid let out a sharp yelp; then Longarm heard him running off down the alley. Longarm ran to the corner of the hotel and peered down the alley that ran behind it. He saw Kincaid vanishing into a doorway farther down. Holding up, Longarm looked quickly around. Kincaid had been too easy to scare off. Longarm wasn't out of the woods yet. Those two Mexicans Kincaid had brought in had to be around here somewhere.

Longarm glanced behind him. A crowd drawn by the gunfire was gathering at the head of the alley. Longarm could hear individual shouts and running feet as the crowd got rapidly larger. Somewhere in back of the crowd a dog began barking.

Longarm cut the other way and started for the rear of Bill Thompson's Feed and Grain Store, heading for his office. There was a shotgun inside, he remembered. Pushing open the door, he found one of the Mexicans waiting for him—the tall, consumptive, cadaverous fellow with the handlebar mustache. He had lit the kerosene lamp and was sitting behind Longarm's desk, waiting for him, the double-barreled shotgun Longarm had come in for resting on the desk in front of him.

The ruse had worked perfectly, Longarm realized. Kincaid had drawn Longarm's fire, then raced off, and Longarm, his guard down, had returned to his office.

The Mexican lifted the shotgun. Longarm ducked to the floor as both barrels thundered. A few pellets swept off Longarm's hat, the rest of the shot pounding into the wall behind him. Drawing his .44, Longarm fired up twice through the desk. The slugs plowed through the dried wood and slapped into living flesh.

The Mexican cried out, then leaped to his feet and staggered out from behind the desk. He was bent over nearly double, both hands clasped frantically about his lower abdomen as he tried to hold his intestines inside his gut where they belonged. Clear of the desk, he

116

sagged onto his knees, then—still holding onto his pulsing entrails—he flopped over onto his side and died.

Running footsteps approached the open door. Longarm turned. The second Mexican entered and pulled up, then paused to stare down at his dead comrade. That pause was fatal. Longarm fired calmly up at the Mexican. Dust rose from his poncho as the slug entered his chest near the solar plexus. The Mexican remained on his feet, however, and fired blindly down at Longarm. The slug smashed through the rotting floorboards inches from Longarm's right boot. Crabbing sideways, Longarm sent another round up into the man. A neat hole appeared in the Mexican's forehaed. He staggered back, hit the wall, then slid down it until he was sitting on the floor, staring at Longarm with wide, unblinking eyes.

Longarm got to his feet and pushed out into the alley. A crowd was surging down the alley toward him. When they saw the smoking gun in his hand, they pulled up. Bursting through the crowd came Jim Gettis, his bodyguards close beside him.

"What happened?" Gettis demanded. "I just saw Kincaid riding out of town. He was wounded, it looked like."

"Two down, one to go."

"You got them two greasers?"

Longarm nodded.

Gettis was about to slap Longarm on the back. Then he pulled back and peered at him. "You need a drink?"

"Yeah. I just lost a near full bottle of Maryland rye."

"Go ahead. I'll see you later at the Long Chance."

Longarm reloaded and dropped his Colt back into his cross-draw rig. Gettis turned to Shorty and told him to get the two bodies out of Long's office, then get rid of them. He didn't care how.

Longarm pushed through the ring of awed townsmen and miners and headed for the Long Chance. He decided he was dry, too damn dry.

Chapter 9

A day later Carlotta knocked lightly on Longarm's open door, then stepped into his office. In the act of hammering a gun rack onto the wall, Longarm put his hammer down and turned to greet Carlotta.

"This is a real pleasure, Carlotta."

"Hello, stranger," she said.

"That's so, and I apologize. But I've been busy."

"So I hear. We been busy too. Have you heard it? Another mine has jus' open."

"I heard. And to everyone's amazement, Jim Gettis doesn't own it."

"Not yet, you mean," Carlotta said, her voice resigned.

He strode over to his desk and slumped down in his swivel chair. Carlotta sat down in the chair beside his desk and took off her sun hat, shaking free her long

119

raven tresses. Her dress was sky blue, with white starched cuffs at each wrist and white lace at her neck. It must have been a hot outfit in this heat, but she looked as cool as a mountain stream.

"It's good to see you again, Carlotta," Longarm said, and meant it.

"Thank you, Custis." She smiled warmly. "I think I been hoping you get chased out of the Long Chance a second time."

"I could move back into the boardinghouse."

"Maybe you should. But now you will have to wait. We have not a room vacant. We are so busy."

"Maybe it's your cooking."

"It is Ventura," she reminded him. "She do most of the cooking."

"This just a social visit, Carlotta?"

She shrugged. "Maybe. But maybe it is not. I wonder, Custis. How much you like this Gettis? Already you kill many men for heem."

"I'm just trying to keep myself alive, Carlotta. It doesn't have anything to do with how I feel about Gettis."

"Then you hate heem, too?"

Longarm shrugged. "He's treated me fairly, Carlotta. I don't hate him."

"You like heem?" She was astonished.

"What do you want me to say, Carlotta?"

"It is not what I want to say. It is what I want you to do!"

"And what might that be?"

"Jim Gettis is the devil! Such a man as you could stop heem!"

Longarm blew out his cheeks. "Maybe so, Carlotta. Maybe I could stop him. And maybe I will. Someday.

Hold off, will you? Give me a chance to make my own moves?"

Hope leaped into her dark eyes. She leaned forward eagerly. "Then you will?"

"I did not say that. I was just asking you to back off—to give me room. Some time. Stop pushing me."

Carlotta looked carefully at Longarm, considering his reply. It was not, she realized, a refusal on Longarm's part to take on Gettis. On the other hand, Longarm had not promised her he would. It was a standoff, and as Longarm returned her gaze, he wondered if he might have said too much. Now was no time to show his hand—no matter how much he might want to placate Carlotta.

Abruptly, Carlotta stood. "All right, Custis," she told him. "I will do as you say. I will not push you. I will give you plenty room." She turned and swept from his office.

Staring after her departing figure, Longarm frowned thoughtfully, wondering if he hadn't at the last of it caught a conspiratorial gleam in Carlotta's eyes—as if in Longarm's guarded response she had grasped, however tentatively, the dilemma he faced.

Late that same day Longarm was relaxing on the porch in front of Bill Thompson's Feed and Grain Store when MacDuff approached. He had evidently been drinking his lunch and had left his hat God knows where and did not seem to be in any great hurry to get back to his editorial post at the *Banner*. Weaving slightly, he paused in his tracks and greeted Longarm.

"Pull up a chair, MacDuff," Longarm offered.

"Don't mind if I do."

He dragged a chair over from the other side of the

121

porch and slumped down into it beside Longarm. Longarm handed him a cheroot, then lit his own and MacDuff's. The editor inhaled deeply, then exhaled luxuriously. Tipping his chair back against the wall, he glanced at Longarm.

"Had a snootful, I did."

"I noticed."

"Only way to fight the damned heat in this corner of hell."

Longarm nodded.

"You got all those new cells built?"

"Yup."

"I don't hear of you arresting any drunks around town. For a town marshal, you ain't all that busy."

"Gettis doesn't think I should be overzealous. A miner can't haul out too much ore if he's sleeping it off in a jail cell."

"And of course you do what Jim Gettis says."

"Why not?"

"I hear he's still out looking for Kincaid."

"That's right. Hang around. Maybe you'll have a good story before sundown."

"A good story would be for Gettis to fall off his horse and split his head open like a watermelon."

Longarm did not bother to reply.

Gettis and his men had been scouring the countryside for two days now. Gettis had not returned yet today and Longarm was waiting for him to do so. As he saw it, he was on the verge of gaining the opportunity he had been seeking. Gettis had assured Longarm that if he apprehended Kincaid, Longarm would be the one to take Kincaid back in irons to the country sheriff who had appointed him. In this eventuality, Longarm would be given the chance he had been waiting for to join forces with Major Danton and move finally on Jim Gettis.

There was no longer any doubt at all in Longarm's mind that Gettis was Sergeant Paul Cable, the army deserter and renegade who had held up that army paymaster six years before. But Gettis was too well-guarded for Longarm to arrest and bring in alone, no matter how close Longarm kept to him and no matter how much Gettis trusted him. In the past few days this had been more and more obvious, and Longarm had finally come to the decision that he would need the help only Major Danton could provide.

"Can't understand it," grumbled MacDuff, shaking his head and peering quizically at Longarm.

"What's that, MacDuff?"

"How a man as decent as you—free with his smokes and willing to share a bottle with a balding newspaper-editor—would be in league with a snake like Jim Gettis. Just can't believe it."

Longarm laughed easily. "Maybe you got poor Jim Gettis all wrong, MacDuff. He might turn out to be the next territorial governor."

"Jesus! Heaven forbid!"

The sound of clattering hooves came to them. Longarm tipped his chair forward and glanced up the street. Jim Gettis, in the midst of at least six dust-covered riders, was approaching, his bodyguards flanking him in front and back as usual. He looked tired, his heavy, lined face grim. When he saw Longarm, he guided his lathered horse toward the hitch rail in front of the feed and grain store. Pulling to a halt, he looped his reins over the saddle horn. But he did not dismount.

"Howdy, Long," he said, nodding curtly to MacDuff, who simply glared back at the man.

"Howdy, Mr. Gettis," Longarm replied. "Any luck?"

"We scared some jackrabbits and rousted some greasers campin' near my land. But Kincaid's long gone. Looks like you done rid us of a real cockroach, Long."

"You sure of that?"

"Hell, yes. And I ain't ridin' after that son of a bitch no more. Not in this heat."

"Sure is hot," Longarm agreed.

"I'm callin' the town council together. We'll have a petition drawn up, stating the case against Kincaid— and *for* you. I figure you bring that to the sheriff in Travis, and he'll make you the new deputy sheriff." He grinned then, his yellow teeth gleaming in his grimy face. "Then we'll have this town *and* the townsite surrounding it by the short hair."

"When do you want me to leave?"

"Tomorrow morning."

"You sure you don't need me to keep track of things here?"

"Hell, what's going to happen? My men can handle any trouble. I want you to see that sheriff as soon as possible. You'll make a good impression. I ain't worried none about that. And I'll have me a new deputy sheriff."

"Okay, Mr. Gettis."

"See me at the Long Chance later tonight. I'll have the petition waiting for you. Leave first thing in the morning. I'll tell the livery to lend you their best horse."

"Thanks."

With a curt nod, ignoring MacDuff completely, Gettis grabbed his reins and started to back his mount away from the hitch rack just as Casey rode into view from the other direction. Catching sight of Gettis, she immediately cut toward him and Gettis's bodyguards pulled their mounts aside to let her through. She was dressed in a dark-brown Stetson, a red silk shirt open at the neck, and a leather split riding skirt. The skirt would have shocked most Easterners; it was not considered proper for a lady to fork a horse like a man. But Casey rode as well as any man, Longarm noticed as she pulled her horse to a halt beside Gettis.

"What the hell're you doin' out in this heat?" Gettis demanded of Casey.

"I've just been out for a ride. You expect me to stay home and bake in that adobe prison you built for me?"

"It ain't no prison—and it's cool."

"No place is cool in this."

"Damn it, Casey. You know I don't like you ridin' out without my say-so."

"You want to discuss this in public, do you? In front of all our friends?" She smiled ironically at Longarm and MacDuff, then swung her gaze at the sullen bodyguards sitting their mounts about them. "Or should we wait till later, when you come over to visit?"

Gettis glanced quickly about him, swallowed his outrage at Casey's independence, and did his best to settle his ruffled feathers. "All right. All right," he told her. "I'll be over soon's I can."

As cool as an icicle, Casey smiled. "I'll have a nice hot bath ready."

"Not too hot," Gettis replied.

Casey urged her horse on past Gettis, lifting it to a lope as she headed for her house at the other end of town, raising a quick, sudden cloud of alkali dust as she went. It hung in the air behind her, no doubt a way for her to show her scorn—and possibly her contempt—for Jim Gettis and his sullen, unwashed crew. Gettis swore as the dust stung at his eyes. He pulled up his kerchief and tugged his hat down over his face, then yanked his horse around and led his men on down the street to the Long Chance.

Longarm watched them go.

"Nice couple, that," commented MacDuff.

"You weren't very polite, editor," Longarm chided. "You could have at least said hello to the man. If you don't watch out, Jim Gettis is going to get the idea you don't like him."

"He knows what I feel about him. That isn't any secret. Not in this town."

"Then watch out, MacDuff," Longarm warned gently as he got to his feet. "Gettis has a short fuse."

"Too bad you don't have as short a fuse—when it comes to dealin' with snakes like him, that is."

Longam was suddenly weary of the editor. He clapped MacDuff on the back, bid him good afternoon, and started across the street toward the barbershop. Casey's mention of a hot bath had reminded him just how much he could use one himself. Then, after some steak and fries at Stella's, he figured he'd stroll around, keep himself out of trouble, and hit the sack early.

Tomorrow would be the day they gave babies away with a half a pound of cheese. It would also be the day he set out for Travis—and Fort Crook. Longarm was satisfied that things were going along about as he had hoped they would. The only trouble was that things never did go entirely as a man planned. He had better keep an eye out for the joker in the deck. Every deck had one.

He dodged an ore truck, gained the porch in front of the barbershop, and ducked inside.

126

• • •

An hour or so after midnight, Longarm was packed and ready for the three-day ride to Travis. The town council's dutifully signed and notarized petition was tucked away safely in his saddlebag, and Longarm was stretched out on his bed, letting the desert's cool night breeze sweep over his naked body.

He was close to dropping off when a soft, urgent knock sounded on his door. He sat up. The knock came again, more insistent this time. He stepped into the bottom half of his long johns and padded on bare feet across the room to the door.

"Who is it?"

"Hurry up and let me in!"

Casey! He turned the key in the lock and pulled the door open. She ducked in past him, smelling as cool as the night wind with only the hint of a very expensive, store-bought fragrance clinging to her. He closed the door and asked a foolish question.

"What do you want, Casey?"

"You mean you really don't know?"

"Besides that, I mean."

She laughed and shook her golden curls out. "Why should I want anything more?" She stepped out of her skirt. There was nothing under it but her, and as she tossed it over the back of a chair she began to unbutton her blouse. When that joined her skirt, she stood proudly before him stark naked, except for her high-button shoes.

"I left the Long Chance early," she explained, sitting on the edge of the bed to unlace her shoes. "I didn't want you to get to sleep before I got here. I took a bath, and this perfume is worth fifty dollars an ounce—at least that's what Jim told me."

"You believe him?"

She kicked off her second shoe and glanced at him. "Never mind that. Just get over here and peel off them long johns." The searing eagerness in her glance was almost enough to strip the long johns off by itself.

"I'm too shy," he told her, joining her on the bed.

"Here then, let me." Her nimble fingers stripped him in an instant.

He was ready for her, she saw. Glancing down at him, her eyes grew large with delight. He moved astride her then, his knees resting on the bed beside her pelvis, his tip poised over her, ready for the plunge.

"What are you waiting for," she gasped. "Go ahead."

"I like some suspense. Don't you?"

"Damn you! Get in there!"

He dropped swiftly, plunging past her moist entrance —and kept on, driving deep into her. When he reached bottom, he pulled back and grinned at her. "How's that?"

Groaning, she thrust upward, slamming into his pelvis. "Yes . . . yes . . . *yes*. That's fine. But don't hold back. Please, Custis. Don't!"

So he didn't.

An hour or so later, still insatiable, she used all her arts to work him back into condition, then clambered up on top of him and plunged down onto his erection. Gasping with delight, she flung her head back, her long golden curls tickling his knees. Then she straightened and began humping. Reaching up, he cupped her breasts in his big, calloused hands. She groaned in ecstasy and began to rotate, slowly at first, then faster. He was still erect and could feel himself deep inside her.

"I wish I could help," he told her. "But I'm done. Drained."

"Just you keep him inside me!" she hissed. "And keep your hands where they are now."

"Yes, ma'am."

Her rotating increased to a maddening pitch, and then she began lifting off him and plunging back down, squealing softly with the pleasure it afforded her. He could hear the pop as she forced out her juices with each plunge as he concentrated on keeping himself up so she wouldn't miss.

And then, gradually at the start, for the third time that night, a white-hot fire began to build in his groin. He grabbed Casey's breasts convulsively, squeezing her bullet-hard nipples. Grinning down at him, she blew a lock of damp hair out of her eyes.

"See!" she panted, her face shining with triumph. "You're coming!"

"You're goddamn right I'm coming! What did you expect?"

"You said you were drained!"

"Shut up . . . and don't stop!"

He grabbed her pelvic bones and, using them as handles, kept her plunging down faster and faster onto him. When he arched his back finally and lifted her high, going off like a cannon deep inside her, she squealed with pleasure, then exploded herself, drenching his crotch and the tops of his thighs. He thought she would never stop coming, but at last she collapsed forward onto him, her arms hugging him, her cheek resting in the thick, curly hair on his chest.

"Mmmm," she murmured, softly. "I do love to fuck you, Mr. Long."

"Don't talk like that."

"I like to talk like that. It makes me feel more wanton. It arouses me. When you hear me, doesn't it arouse you?"

"It shocks me," he said, grinning.

"I don't care," she sighed.

And in that moment she was not a tough, hard-eyed gambler, mistress to a ruthless gang leader, but instead a happy young lady having a wonderful time behind her pa's barn, when nothing that felt so good could possibly be wrong.

He stroked her long, damp curls.

"I got to get up early tomorrow," he told her.

"I know."

"What about you? Shouldn't you get back? After you ridin' out like that today, your lord and master might even send one of his men over to your place tomorrow morning to keep an eye on you."

"Don't worry. I wore him out plenty this afternoon, sweetened the bastard up real good."

"I think the word for you is insatiable."

"There's another word for me, too."

"And what might that be?"

"Desperate."

"Maybe you better explain that."

"Remember the last time I visited you?"

"Of course."

"I told you I wanted my freedom. You said I was like a bird in a cage."

"I got carried away."

"Well, that's what you said, and you were right. You saw Jim today. You heard him. He doesn't want me to leave this place. Ever. I cannot even ride out on my own without his permission. I am his prisoner."

"Ah, but Casey, you are a prisoner of love."

"Love! That pig! You think I could love that man?"

Her vehemence chastened him. "Easy, Casey. I was just kidding."

"If I love anyone, it would be you. *You* are a man! And I think maybe you'll be the man to save me."

Longarm came alert quickly. "All right, Casey. What are you leading up to?"

"You're riding out of here tomorrow. Is that not true?"

"It is."

"You are going to Travis."

"That's right."

"I want you to take me with you."

"Take you *with* me? I can't do that, Casey."

"Why not? Because you are afraid of Jim?"

"Shouldn't I be?"

"You won't have anything to fear from him. He will not connect you to my disappearance."

"And how will you manage that?"

"I will ride out tonight alone and meet you later at Indian Wells. That's on the way to Travis, about ten miles out. I'll go that far in my buggy, carrying provisions and trailing extra horses. How can Jim possibly connect my disappearance with you?"

"By adding two and two."

"Please, Custis. Everything is ready. My buggy, the provisions, and my horses."

"Then do it. Why do you need to involve me? Why not just ride out on your own?"

She sighed unhappily. "I could do that, of course. I know how to get to Indian Wells. But farther than that is out of the question. More than once I've tried to cross that country, but there're no landmarks. It's as flat as the top of a stove—and just as hot. I'll need your help to get to Travis. Then you'll be rid of me. I promise, Custis."

Longarm shook his head. "Gettis won't let you go, Casey. You'll never reach Travis. He'll be after you before the day is out."

"No, he won't."

"Why won't he?"

"Why do you think I'm leaving now, Custis?"

"All right. I give up. Why?"

"Jim won't be back here for a couple of days at least. When he was searching for Kincaid, he discovered some Mexicans moving onto his land west of here, and he's gone after them with his bullyboys. Then he's cutting south across the border to help himself to some cattle."

"That's where he gets his stock?"

She nodded. "He's got some Apaches on his payroll. They love to show the white man how they take from the Mexicans whatever they need. That'll give us two, maybe three days. We'll be in Travis by then, and before he catches up to us, I'll be on my way to California."

"Leaving me to handle Gettis."

"Custis, why on earth should he blame you for my disappearance? Everyone will testify that you rode out alone. Besides, I'll leave Jim a note. I've been threatening to light out for months now, and in the note I'll tell him I've gone back to my folks in Kansas. Besides, as far as he knows, we're hardly acquainted."

Longarm considered her words carefully, then nodded. "Well, if no one sees us together."

"Then you'll take me with you?"

Longarm pondered a moment, then shrugged. "I could take you as far as Travis, I suppose. So long as we don't ride into Travis together and we keep apart while you're waiting for the stage."

With a squeal of delight she flung her arms around his neck. "You'll see! I won't let anyone see us together, but I promise, we'll have a wonderful time saying good-bye to each other! There're some tricks I haven't shown you yet."

He grinned at her. "I can imagine."

She got up from the bed and dressed quickly, her eyes alight, humming softly to herself. It was clear now why she had visited him this night. She had used all her wiles and her considerable skills as a woman to soften him up, to convince him to help her, and she was delighted with her success. He went with her to the door. She hugged him, thanked him again, then vanished down the hallway. He waited until her footsteps had faded completely on the back stairs before closing the door behind her.

Longarm returned to his bed and lay back down, his arms crossed under his head, and did some long thinking. If anything could draw Jim Gettis out of his lair, make him overplay his hand—it would be Casey. Which meant a lot could happen between Copper City and Travis. Casey was a wild card he had been dealt, and it wasn't clear how Longarm was going to play her. But she was sure as hell going to make the game interesting.

Meanwhile, he'd better keep his powder dry and his ass down.

Chapter 10

Casey entered the rear of the Long Chance on cat feet and glided past Calder's office to the next door past it, the one leading to Calder's own living quarters. She remembered the room as a narrow cubicle with a single bed against the far wall, a cluttered dresser and a commode. Once, in order to gain a favor, she had allowed Calder to have his way with her. It had not been pleasant, and now, as she stood outside the door with her ear against the panel, she could almost feel Calder's cadaverous arms clinging to her like the branches of a dead tree.

When she heard Kincaid's booted feet come up behind her and pause, she rapped softly on Calder's door. She heard the sudden squeak of a bedspring.

"Who's there?" Calder asked, his voice low, cautious.

"It's me. Casey."

She heard the man's bare feet padding toward the door, then the sound of his key turning in the lock. As Calder pulled back the door, Kincaid brushed swiftly past her and flung the door open wide. There was a revolver in Calder's right hand, but he was too astonished to raise it. As he staggered back, Kincaid brought the barrel of his revolver down on the top of the man's skull. Calder crumpled to the floor without a sound and did not move.

Moving past the body, Casey pulled open the drawer in the night table by Calder's bed and pulled forth the office keys. She left the room with them, and while she was opening the office door, Kincaid—Calder's unconscious body slung over his shoulder—moved past her and disappeared into the back alley.

When he returned and stepped into the office behind her, Casey was just pulling open the safe's door. She had watched Calder open the safe often enough and had long since memorized the combination. Kincaid had several grain sacks with him, and into these they transferred the pouches of gold coins. As they worked, Kincaid's eyes gleamed as he noted the size of the haul. The safe was full, since it was only a few days before Gettis was supposed to send the gold to his bank in Travis, a deposit he made twice a month.

They did not fill the grain sacks, since that would be too much for them to haul at a time. Even so, after dividing the gold evenly between four of the sacks, it still took both of them working together to lug each sack out and load it under the seat in Casey's buggy.

That accomplished, Casey returned to the office, closed the safe, then locked the office door behind her. She then hurried into Calder's room, made his bed as carelessly as was Calder's habit, gathered up his gun belt and revolver, his hat, boots, trousers, and frock coat, then locked the door behind her and left.

For the next day's business, the barkeeps would run the saloon without Calder's presence. They had done this often enough in the past. Anyone looking for Calder would simply assume he had left on business of his own. The head barkeep, having a key to the office, would deposit the night's take on Calder's office table as was his custom and then lock the door behind him. There was no danger he would notice the safe had been cleaned out, since he did not have the safe's combination and would have no reason to open it anyway.

The unconscious Calder had already been thrown unceremoniously onto the floorboards behind the buggy's seat, and Kincaid was sitting up on it with the reins in his hand. Dumping Calder's clothing beside him, Casey stepped up onto the seat beside Kincaid.

"Let's go."

He nodded and slapped the reins smartly over the backs of the two horses. Under his hat brim, a portion of the clean white bandage Casey had wrapped about his head earlier that day was visible. Longarm's bullet had creased Kincaid's skull and the wound had bled profusely, but Casey had nursed him through it, then hidden him in a ravine outside of town, where she had taken him as soon as Gettis and his men had thoroughly searched it. She had been coming from the ravine when she rode into town and met Gettis returning from the hunt.

Now, as she rode through the cool night toward her house, she found herself tingling with excitement. At last she was getting out of this miserable, scalding place! And with a fortune, to boot. Gettis's own money!

Of course, she knew it might all go bad. She might end up with a bullet in her back—or worse. But that didn't matter. She was making her move after many long bitter years. And what she felt as a result was a wild and unabashed exultation at the prospect.

Only a small tiny voice within her chided her for the cruel trick she had in mind for Kincaid.

Her house was dark. She had given the Mexican housekeeper and her husband, the gardener, the week off to visit their children. Grateful for this unexpected kindness, they had piled into their ancient wagon and left that evening. Kincaid carried the still-unconscious Calder into the house and dumped him on Casey's bed. She placed Calder's clothes beside him, hanging his gun belt and holster over one of the bedposts at the foot of the bed. Except for the lower half of his long johns, Calder was naked, but Casey made no effort to dress him. He was still unconscious, and seeing this, Casey leaned close to make sure he was still breathing.

He was.

Stepping back, she nodded to Kincaid. Using rope he had brought in with him, Kincaid bound the man securely to the bedposts, then shoved the corner of a towel into his mouth, securing it with a short length of rope he wound about the man's head. As Kincaid stepped back to inspect his handiwork, Calder's eyes flickered open, then focused with naked terror upon Casey and Kincaid. Calder tried to say something, then gave it up. His attempts to get loose from the rope holding him were equally futile.

Casey leaned close.

"Listen, Calder, tell Jim I've left him for good. Kincaid's going home to Texas, and I'm going with him.

138

Jim can come after us if he wants, but Texas is a big state. So long."

The man seemed enormously relieved that they were not going to pop him again. He nodded quickly at Casey, tiny beads of cold sweat standing out on his forehead.

Casey turned to Kincaid. "Let's go," she said, stepping past him.

With a quick nod, Kincaid followed her from the bedroom. Outside on the porch, she paused to glance up at the stars. From the position of the dipper, she could see that it was only a few hours after midnight. There was plenty of time for them to reach Indian Wells before Long got there.

"Wait a minute," Kincaid said behind her. "I left my hat."

He ducked back into the house and strode into the bedroom and found his hat on one of the bedposts. He clapped on the hat, then bent over Calder's bound figure. The man looked up at him with quizzical, frightened eyes. Kincaid drew his revolver and brought its barrel down on the top of Calder's head with every ounce of strength he had. Calder's skull broke like a rotten eggshell. Kincaid smiled. Calder wouldn't be telling Jim Gettis what Casey had just told him. He wouldn't be telling anyone a damn thing.

Holstering his gun, Kincaid left the room.

Casey had already stepped up into her buggy and had the reins in her hand when he stepped out onto the porch and straightened his hat. She glanced at him impatiently.

"We haven't much time."

"I know it," he told her shortly.

He stepped off the porch and headed for the barn to get the two saddle horses. A moment later, the horses trailing behind the buggy, they rode from the yard. As they turned onto the road leading out of town, Casey did not once glance back at what had been her home for so many years.

It was mid-morning when Casey sighted the red bluffs of Indian Wells in the distance. During the first months of spring, fed by the snowmelt in the mountains to the west, Indian Wells was the lush, even fertile, confluence of two hard-flowing streams. For the rest of the year, however, Indian Wells was at best a rapidly dwindling water hole that by the end of the summer had shrunk under the sun's cruel gaze to little more than a damp mudhole. A mile long pine-topped bluff, its weathered flanks red in the hot sun and visible for miles, reared up behind Indian Wells.

Already weary and bone dry from the pitiless sun's blast, Casey breathed a sigh of relief at sight of the distant bluff. Glancing back at her horses she saw they were not laboring. But the horses pulling the buggy— and the four sacks of gold it contained—were in some distress. Not only were they laboring, but dried lather streaked their flanks. They would make it to Indian Wells, however. She was sure of that. And at this time of year there would be enough water to revive them— and during the wait for Long to show, they would have plenty of time to get their strength back.

So far, so good, she told herself.

"How's your wound?" she asked Kincaid.

"Throbs a little."

"I'll take a look at it soon's we get a chance."

"It don't need no more lookin' at. You already done fixed it fine."

"Have it your way."

Kincaid had said hardly a word since leaving Copper City. His heavy silences did not bother her, however. She was confident she could handle the man. Dealing with him had been no more difficult than with any other man. Hell, she mused, when it came time for her to meet the devil, she would have something to offer him, as well.

What had assured her of Kincaid's assistance from the start was her offer to deliver Custis Long to him—that, plus a quarter of the gold they took from Gettis's safe. Strangely enough she had found that, of all the inducements she had offered Kincaid, her plan to help him even the score with Custis Long seemed by far the most important—even more important, she realized, than her offer of herself as a bonus once they arrived safely in Travis.

But Casey was under no illusions about Kincaid.

He was a sullen, dangerous man. For that reason, she kept a trump up her sleeve—or rather strapped to her thigh. It was a pearl-handled Smith & Wesson .32 revolver, a weapon she could reach in an instant through the slit she had sewn in her skirt. Jim Gettis had long since taught her how to use the revolver, and she was as confident of her aim with it as any gunslick that rode beside Gettis.

Of course, she had no intention whatsoever of sharing her wealth with Kincaid, and she would certainly not allow him to shoot Custis. Her plan from the beginning had been to draw on Kincaid the moment Long showed up. She was confident that when Custis saw the gold she had taken, he would forget any loyalty he might feel toward Gettis, deal summarily with Kincaid, then take off with her to San Francisco. And that would only be the beginning. From San Francisco they would set sail for the great capitals of the world.

It was a fabulous dream, one that grew wilder and more extravagant with each successive embellishment —but Casey was determined to make this dream a reality, and had already taken the first steps in that direction.

There was plenty of water for the horses, and after filling his canteen and emptying it over his head, Kincaid slumped back against a slab of rock and watched Casey bathe her face and neck as she leaned out over the water hole using a handkerchief she was forced to wring out constantly. To wash her arms, she had slipped off her blouse, so that above her waist she wore only her shift.

"Why don't you take the rest of your clothes off and dive in?" Kincaid suggested, leering.

"It would drive you wild and then where would we be?"

"It would sure as hell do that. Do you think maybe we could do it standing up in the water?"

"Sounds like a wonderful idea. But not right now."

He studied her closely for a moment and she could tell from the way his eyes fed on her bare shoulders and cleft that he was considering whether or not to jump her. After all, there was no one around to stop him. She pulled back from the edge of the water hole and waited, her hand resting lightly on the ground beside the slit in her skirt.

Abruptly, Kincaid shrugged, took out his sack of Bull Durham and built himself a cigarette.

She finished cleaning off her face and arms, stood up, and slipped her blouse back over her head. Tucking it in, she looked around. Above them towered the bluff, less than forty paces away. The buggy was parked in its shadow, the four horses cropping what grass there was at its base. The sky beyond the bluff was cloudless and milk white in the hard, unrelenting glare of the sun. She turned back around and gazed across the water hole back the way they had come, wondering how many hours it would take before Long arrived. Four, maybe five hours, at least. Maybe she could go back to the bluff, find a shady spot, and take a nap, After all, she had been going full out since the previous day.

As she had explained it to Kincaid, her plan was to ride out to greet Long as soon as he showed, then ride back with him, keeping him properly distracted until Kincaid could blow him away. In other words, she was to be the Judas Goat that delivered Long into Kincaid's hands. Of course, she had no intention of doing anything of the kind—as soon as she saw Long, she would take out her Smith & Wesson and disarm Kincaid. Even as she thought this, she reached down to feel the .32 revolver's clean outline in its holster strapped to her thigh. Of course, it wouldn't do any good, she realized, if she didn't keep herself awake, to be ready when Long appeared.

But it sure wouldn't hurt any to get out of this sun.

"I'm going back to the bluff," she told him. "I'll keep an eye on the horses and maybe find a grassy spot."

"Sure," Kincaid said. "Good idea."

He spoke without looking at her as he drew on his cigarette and squinted into the distance. He was pretty damned anxious, she realized, to get Custis Long in his sights.

Despite her best intentions, as soon as she found a comfortable spot in the grass below the bluff, she fell asleep. A shadow shifting between her and the sun aroused her. She opened her eyes and found not one, but three men standing over her. Two Mexicans and Kincaid. Behind them she saw four mules. The Mexicans were grinning down at her, taking her measure.

Oh, God! she thought. *It's all coming apart!*

Doing her best to hide her alarm, she smiled and sat up. "Who're your friends, Kincaid?"

"Hipachi Leon's brothers. They've come to help me avenge Hipachi's killer."

"You sure you need them?"

"Don't you think they got the right?"

"I guess so. Sure. I'm just surprised, that's all. You never mentioned them to me."

"You never asked. I sent for them after you fixed my head wound."

"I was just thinking of the gold. I mean I didn't figure on splitting it four ways."

He smiled. "Neither did I. I still don't."

He was mocking her, playing with her, really. It was in his tone of voice, the sudden insolent gleam in his eyes. The two Mexicans stepped closer and smiled down at her. In their eyes she was already naked. She knew that when they took her, they would be rough, snorting and laughing and rutting like drunken Indians. Worse even than Jim Gettis. Her dreams of voyaging to Europe with Custis, of shopping with him in Paris even, were gone instantly as she saw with cruel clarity how foolish and impossible such dreams had been.

Her only hope now was not to panic, to act calm, not

to show them the fear she felt. After all, she still had her .32.

"Ain't you going to introduce me to your friends?" she asked, leaning casually back against the bluff's wall.

"Sure," Kincaid said, grinning in anticipation of what he knew was to come. "The one on my right is Miguel, the other one is Panchito. But he ain't all that small. Not where it counts, anyway."

She brushed her hair off her forehead as she squinted up at Kincaid. "There's a look in your eye, Kincaid. I don't like it. Am I supposed to entertain your friends?"

"Sure. But I go first."

He took a step closer.

"No," she said, stalling. "Not here. Can't we find a more comfortable spot?"

"Just what I was thinking," Kincaid said, pulling up. "I noticed a cleft in the wall up there a ways. There's plenty of grass inside, even some clover."

She pushed herself upright. "All right," she said.

She started ahead of them along the base of the bluff, heading for the cleft Kincaid had mentioned, hoping desperately that the Mexicans didn't lose control and grab her before they reached the place—and she was ready to make her move. When she came to the cleft, she entered ahead of them, striding forward quickly in order to get a few yards ahead of them. As soon as she felt she had the room she needed, she reached into the slit in her skirt for the Smith & Wesson.

Only it wasn't there!

Grinning, Kincaid halted and pulled the .32 out of his side pocket and held it up for her to see. The revolver gleamed like a kid's toy in his big hand.

"This what you're lookin' for?" he asked. "You were

real tired, Casey. You slept like a babe. Didn't even stir when I took this from your holster."

In a shaky voice, she asked, "You knew I had it?"

"I brushed against it when we were loading them sacks of gold. I figured if you didn't let on you had it, you must be plannin' some sort of surprise."

"All right, Kincaid! You got the gun, so that gives you the advantage. But I ain't servicing these greasers —nor you, either. Just take the gold and clear out."

"Oh, we'll take the gold, Casey. Don't worry none about that. But we're gonna take you too, we're gonna plow you raw, Casey. Then we'll finish off that bastard, Long."

"Damn you!" she seethed. "Damn you all to hell!"

His grin widened. "You know what, Casey? I'm thinking this ain't at all what you had in mind. Am I right?"

She turned and ran, cut around a boulder, saw a narrow lane leading deep into the bluff, and kept on going. Rounding another boulder, she almost slammed full tilt into a sheer wall of rock extending nearly straight up. Like a small animal too terrified to think clearly, she tried to scale it, her fingers clawing at the steep, ribbed surface. She got no higher than a few feet before the Mexicans overtook her, grabbed her roughly from behind, then flung her brutally to the ground. There was little grass here, nothing to shield her from the rocks embedded into the ground that dug cruelly into her back and buttocks.

They flung up her skirt and tore off her undergarments. She closed her eyes and tried not to think of what was happening.

She sat a few feet from the water hole, her back against a boulder, hugging her drawn-up knees, watching the three men. Her lips were swollen, and bruises purpled each cheekbone. The beating had come when she tried to stop the three of them from going around for a second time. She had not been successful. But that was past now, and they were done with her, content to peer into the shimmering distance and wait for Long to show.

The gold the Mexicans had already packed in aparejos on the mules they had brought. The two Mexicans were obviously anxious to get moving. All that gold made them nervous. But they were excited as well. They talked incessantly of the tequila they were going to drink and the whores they were going to buy. And every now and then they would glance over at her and grin as they remembered.

She almost wished she were back in her adobe prison in Copper City.

Almost.

"I think maybe I see heem," said Panchito, pointing.

The others leaned quickly forward and peered at the horizon. At first Casey could see only the wavering double horizon until, finally, a kind of ghostly horse and rider appeared and disappeared as if they were suspended just above the horizon. After a while the image became more solid, but even so, it appeared that the horse and rider were moving through a distant, shimmering lake.

"It's him all right," said Kincaid.

The two Mexicans grinned and drew their side arms, checked their loads, then jammed them back into their holsters. Then they picked up their rifles and glanced inquiringly at Kincaid. He nodded. They got to their feet and glided swiftly off toward the bluff.

Kincaid levered a fresh cartridge into his Winchester's firing chamber, then glanced at Casey. "Looks like your friend Long is riding right into our little trap."

She shrugged. "I don't give a damn about Long—not if you promise to take me with you."

"Sure," Kincaid told her, laughing. "I'll take you with me."

"Promise!"

"All right. I promise."

She knew he was lying through his teeth, but that didn't matter. "Then I'm going back to the bluff," she informed him. "I don't want to see this."

"Your deal was to ride out and meet Long, bring him in closer so I'd get a better shot."

"Not now. You won't get me to do that now."

"Why so squeamish all of a sudden?"

"It's what you and your friends just did. I know now what it feels like to be betrayed."

"Hell, Casey, admit it! You loved every minute of it. What does it matter to you, anyway? Once the bread's been cut, who's going to miss a few more slices?"

"You going to let me get back out of this?"

"Go ahead," he said, snorting contemptuously at her qualms. "This won't take long—not with Miguel and Panchito up there. Best two men with a rifle I've ever seen."

Casey got up and hurried back to the bluff, found a spot beside her buggy, and slumped down onto the cool grass. Looking beyond Kincaid she could see Long approaching. He and the horse he was riding were no longer wavering. Horse and rider were growing more solid now with each passing second. She wondered how many yards off he was by this time. It was almost impossible to judge distances in this heat.

One of her saddle horses, cropping the grass beside her, whickered softly. She turned to look at it. The animal raised its head from the grass and returned her gaze, its ears flickering questioningly. She snapped her fingers softly and at once it threw up its head and trotted toward her. She had ridden bareback as a child, and once or twice in the years since. But it was not something she did as a rule. It was not that easy.

Her heart pounding, she reached out and patted the horse's long cheek. It moved closer, its head nudging her shoulder. She wrapped her arms around its neck and looked back at Kincaid. His back was to her, intent on Long as he lay beside one of the boulders shielding the water hole. His rifle was out in front of him, and as she watched, he lifted it and sighted along the barrel.

Long was so close now, she could see the sunlight glinting off his horse's bit.

Abruptly, he pulled his mount to a halt. Cursing softly, Kincaid lowered his rifle.

Longarm peered at the bluff, patting his mount's neck to make it stand quietly. Yes. He was sure of it now. Casey's buggy was parked against the base of the bluff, well back of the water hole. In the shimmering heat waves, he could barely make out the water hole itself and the pile of boulders surrounding it. But the red bluff behind it was clear enough, almost as if he were peering at it through binoculars.

If Casey was here—as that buggy indicated—and was waiting for him as she had promised she would be, why hadn't she called out to him by this time? He and his mount were the only living creatures moving across

149

a vast, searing tabletop of a desert floor. It would be impossible for her not to have seen him by this time. So why hadn't she? No sooner did Longarm pose the question than he knew the answer.

Someone—or something—was keeping Casey from riding out to greet him.

Leaning forward quickly, he snaked his Winchester out of its sling and dismounted. Then he slapped his mount on the rear smartly enough to send it trotting vigorously toward a dry wash a few hundred yards to Longarm's right. Keeping to any cover that offered itself, from dry washes and clumps of mesquite to dunes of pure white sand, he advanced with great care on the water hole, his eyes focused on the rocks and boulders surrounding it. He saw no one. Wondering at last if his precautions were unnecessary, the product perhaps of an overworked imagination, he straightened up cautiously and kept on, trotting in full view at times, his rifle still at the ready.

He heard the sudden clatter of distant hooves, and above it a barely audible shout.

Flinging himself flat behind a mesquite bush, he peered through it to see Casey, astride a sleek black saddle horse, galloping out past the water hole. She was riding bareback, and as she got closer, she cried out again. This time Longarm was able—just barely—to hear her.

"Go back, Custis! Go back! It's a trap!"

A rifle shot rang out form the rocks near the water hole. Longarm saw Casey slump forward, but she wrapped her arms around the horse's neck and kept on riding. Another shot came then, this one from the bluff above. A slug exploded in the sand inches from his foot. He knew he should pull back, but Casey was still on the horse, still riding toward him.

As the air became alive with singing lead, he waited for her to reach him, and when she did, he stepped forward and caught her as she slumped sideways off the horse. The animal swerved wildly, then galloped back toward the bluff in a nervous zigzag. Longarm pulled Casey into a gully deep enough, he hoped, to shield them from the gunfire. Casey's face was a mess. Her lips were swollen and there were ugly bruises on her cheekbones. She was wearing no blouse, only her shift, and her skirt was torn.

She smiled wanly up at him. "I had to warn you."

"What the hell's going on?"

"I used Kincaid to help me get Jim's gold. That's him back there with two of his Mexican buddies. They've been waiting for you."

"You mean before you left, you took the gold in Gettis's safe?"

"Yes."

"Who the hell's idea was that?"

"Mine."

"Jesus, Casey."

She nodded. "I know. It was crazy. And it . . . didn't go the way I planned, Custis."

She began to cough then. He rolled her over gently to see how badly she had been hit. There was a long, ugly wound in her back. The slug had entered high, then apparently ranged down clear to her kidneys. There was no exit wound that he could see, which meant the slug was still lodged in her back somewhere. He rolled her gently back.

"Damn it all, Casey," he chided. "You should have stayed back there instead of riding out here."

"I couldn't let you ride into a trap. I had to warn you."

He left her to move up the wash and peer over its lip at the water hole. On the rim of the bluff two men stood out clearly against the sky. Peering back down at the water hole, Longarm finally made out the head and shoulders of someone working his way toward him. Kincaid, moving with great care, keeping his head down as he darted from mesquite bush to gully.

Longarm went back to Casey.

"What's their disposition?" he asked her. "What am I up against?"

She had to moisten her cracked lips to reply. "There're two Mexicans on the bluff," she managed. "Kincaid's near the water hole."

"Not now he isn't."

"What do you mean?"

"I mean he's coming out here after us."

"Get him, Long. Please. Get him for me."

He patted her on the hand. "I'll see what I can do."

Carefully this time, he inched out of the gully and, keeping his ass and head down, crawled forward in a direction calculated to intercept the approaching Kincaid. When Longarm caught sight of Kincaid again, the man was much closer, heading right for him. Since he had not drawn fire, he was getting just a mite reckless. He was no longer so careful about using cover and was keeping his head up as he searched for sign of Longarm.

Longarm dropped into a small hollow of sand and kept perfectly still as he fitted the Winchester's stock to his shoulder. Lifting the barrel, he caught Kincaid's head and shoulders in his front sight. He was about to squeeze off his shot when he heard a familiar, unnerving sound close beside him. He caught a slight movement out of the corner of his eye and, shifting his head a fraction, he found himself staring into the cold eyes of a rattler. It was lifting its head less than three feet from him. A young snake with only a small complement of rattles, it was making up in enthusiasm what it lacked in experience.

Longarm rolled swiftly away, then broke from cover. Leaping to his feet, he decided he had no choice now but to make a virtue out of necessity and raced full tilt toward the startled Kincaid, who came to a sudden start and flung up his rifle. With his stock resting on his hip, Longarm fired and levered rapidly, keeping up a steady fusilade as he rushed toward Kincaid.

One of Longarm's bullets found its target and Kincaid howled in pain and spun to the ground. But he was not out of action. As he struck the ground, he snapped off two quick shots at Longarm. The bullets went wild, but then, from the top of the mesa, a rapid fusilade of rifle fire commenced, chewing up the ground about Longarm.

Longarm turned and raced back the way he had come, leaping for cover behind a mesquite-crowned ridge. Burrowing into its bank, he let the riflemen on the bluff empty their magazines at him. For a while the bombardment was fierce and intimidating, showering him with sand and mesquite. When the fusilade finally ran out of steam, Longarm peered up over the ridge in time to see Kincaid limping past the rocks above the water hole, then disappear in the direction of the bluff. A few minutes after, Longarm heard the fading clatter of hooves and realized that Kincaid and his Mexicans had decided it would be wiser to make off with the gold than to continue this duel with Longarm.

It was a standoff, Longarm realized. Thanks to Casey.

He returned to where he had left her. She was still on her back, her head turned away from him. His heart sank, however, when he saw the absence of color in her cheeks. Kneeling beside her, he rested the back of his hand against her cheek and turned her head. Her eyes were open wide as she stared at him. But she didn't see him—or anything else that belonged to this world.

Reaching over, he gently closed her eyes.

Only a few minutes before, Casey had asked him to get Kincaid for her. From this moment on, as far as he was concerned, that request was an order. He had been sent here by Billy Vail to bring in Jim Gettis.

But apprehending that renegade sergeant would just have to wait.

Chapter 11

Gettis returned to Silver City the day after Longarm left for Travis—a full two days before Casey had expected him to do so.

The Mexican squatters that Gettis and his men had gone after had fled before they arrived, possibly because word had reached them of the summary manner in which Gettis had dealt with the others he had found a few days earlier. Gettis had then decided to send his foreman and four of his best hands into Mexico for the cattle without him.

Gettis was eager to return to Copper City—and Casey.

The truth of it was that Gettis was still buzzing from the good time Casey had given him before he had ridden out two days before. He wanted a repeat performance. And just as soon as he could get it. Casey's wild and abandoned love-making had not only pleased him, it had profoundly gratified him, reawakenig his old passion for her. Indeed, its intensity had given him a new appreciation of his own masculinity, for there was little doubt in his mind that it was his own powerful, vigorous presence that had so aroused Casey.

It was a little after six in the evening when he arrived back at Copper City. He rode directly to the Long Chance and dismounted. As Gettis pushed into the saloon with Shorty and Mac, Slim took their horses on down-street to the livery.

When he did not see Casey at her faro table, Gettis pulled up. He was surprised, but not alarmed. She was probably in his office prettying herself up before coming out. It was early yet. His two bodyguards following close behind him, he pushed through the early-evening crush and strode over to the head barkeep, Fowler.

"Where's Calder?" Gettis asked the man. "He around?"

Fowler put down the bottle he had been pouring from and shrugged. "I don't know, Jim. He didn't come in this morning. He didn't come in yesterday, either."

"What's that?"

"I ain't seen him in two days, Jim, not since you left. I checked his room. Bed's made, but his boots and side arm are missing. Must be off somewhere."

"Where's last night's take?"

"It's sitting on the table where we left it in his office." Fowler took a key out of his apron pocket and handed it to Gettis. "Here's the key. The take from last night's still in there on the table."

"You mean it ain't been counted out yet?"

Fowler shrugged nervously. "Like I said, Jim, Calder

ain't been in, not since you left." The barkeep smiled hopefully. "Maybe he's visitin' that Mexican chick he took a liking to last month."

"She ditched him," Gettis said shortly.

"Didn't know that, Jim."

"You got the key to his private room there, too?"

The barkeep reached back for the key and handed it to Gettis, who took it and started to push himself away from the bar. Pausing, he glanced back at the barkeep. "Casey in my office, is she?"

The barkeep's face pale. Gettis felt a sudden sick emptiness in the pit of his stomach.

"She ain't been in either, Jim," the barkeep said. He cleared his throat nervously. "Not since you left."

Gettis felt the blood draining from his face. But he knew he shouldn't panic. He was just jumping to conclusions. He let his gaze sweep the room, as if Casey and Calder had been here all this time and were only waiting for the right moment to pop up and surprise him. But the only familiar faces he recognized belonged to the few miners and freighters he knew personally. As they met his gaze, they lifted their beer mugs to him in salute, grinning idiotically.

My God, he thought. *Do they know?*

He turned away, his scalp tightening, a dryness in his mouth. Though he kept telling himself he had nothing to worry about, that Casey not being here and Calder's disappearance had a perfectly reasonable explanation, he felt as if he were caught up in a nightmare. He nodded woodenly to Shorty and Mac. They turned about the preceded him into the back hallway.

Unlocking the door and stepping into Calder's room, Gettis saw the bed made up in Calder's usual indifferent way. A quick check in the closet showed his boots,

157

coat, and trousers were missing, and as the barkeep had mentioned, Calder had taken his gun belt and revolver, not that the man would ever dare use the thing. His mind racing at a fearsome clip, Gettis tried to keep himself under control, to find the sense of it without panicking.

Calder was little more than the shadow of the man who had been running this saloon when Gettis first rode into Copper City. He had offered little resistance to Gettis's demand that he sell out, willing to give up his ownership and settle for running the place, content to wait for the consumption that had dogged him this far to take him. Apart from this saloon, he had no real life of his own. It was all he knew or cared about. In his condition he had some difficulty maintaining an interest in women, which was why that Mexican girl had left him, complaining to Casey that Calder was bloodless and no real man.

So if he *had* gone off with Casey, why in hell would he do such a thing? And a damn sight better question would be what had possessed Casey to take off with Calder? Hell! She could barely tolerate the man.

Slow down. Slow down. Maybe she hadn't gone off with him. Maybe he would find Casey at the house drunk out of her mind, too damn pissed off with the heat to want to work these two days. And maybe Calder had found himself another Mexican chick, after all, and not expecting Gettis back this soon, was off proving his manhood.

Gettis's heart pounded hopefully at this thought as he left Calder's room and opened the office door. Inside, he saw the sacks of gold and other currencies from the night before lined up neatly on the table. The ledger rested in its rack above it. The swivel chairs and three hard-backed wooden chairs waited in their accustomed places.

Except that the chair next to the safe had been pushed to one side.

"Damn!" Gettis said softly. Kneeling quickly in front of the safe, he flicked the tumblers, heard the click, then pulled open the door. *Empty!* He sat back on his haunches and stared grimly into the safe's yawning emptiness.

So that was it!

He stood up and took a deep breath. Half a month's take was but a trickle in the golden flow he realized from his various enterprises, and he could make up this loss in less than a month, putting it behind him with barely a qualm. But what sickened him was not the robbery. It was Casey's betrayal. He would not find her waiting in the house for him, drunk. And Calder was not shacking up with any Mexican pig. Somehow, Casey had managed to convince that half-dead Calder to help her rob Gettis and then run off with her.

Shorty and Mac had entered the office and were standing beside him, both men peering past Gettis at the empty safe. They knew perfectly well what had happened. They turned their gaze on Gettis, their eyes gleaming with eagerness, like hounds waiting to be cut loose.

"That son of a bitch, Calder," Shorty said, hitching up his pants and swelling out his chest. "We'll track the bastard, boss. He won't get far. Not with that load to carry."

Mac nodded quickly in agreement. Both men, it seemed, were in accord in believing that Johnny Calder had taken the gold and skipped.

"Keep this quiet, both of you," Gettis commanded,

kicking the safe door shut and waving them both ahead of him out of the room.

As soon as they reached the hallway, he turned and locked the door, pocketed the keys, and pushed past them down the hallway and into the saloon. Striding ahead of his two bodyguards out of the place, he met Slim returning from the livery. Without a word to him, Gettis turned down the street and, squinting through the windblown sand, headed on foot toward Casey's house, his three bodyguards following close behind him. The fourth member of his team of bodyguards had gone with Gettis's foreman to Mexico, and at that moment Gettis was sorry he had let him go.

He might need him. The world he had so carefully built here in this town was coming unstuck, and his sense of disaster was growing. It felt as if he had been punched repeatedly in the stomach. And the worse part of it was he had no choice but to continue to walk upright past the staring eyes, tell no one what he felt, and keep going.

Gettis slumped back down in the easy chair and looked dazedly at the figure still bound hand and foot to the bedposts. His stomach was churning, and he could feel a painful band tightening about his forehead. Slim, Mac, and Shorty were standing at the foot of the bed, peering in dumb wonder at Calder's corpse.

"Jesus," Shorty said softly after a moment.

"The poor son of a bitch," said Mac. The big man hunched his shoulders nervously, then glanced over at Gettis.

"Guess it wasn't him stole that gold," ventured Slim, moistening his lips. "That right, boss?"

"Get him out of here," snapped Gettis. "Wrap him in

160

those blankets, dig a hole out near the barn and bury the son of a bitch. It won't matter to him where he sleeps, not now. And I don't want any word of this to get out."

The three men took deep unhappy breaths and approached the bed from the side. When they paused, it was the sight of Calder's shattered skull that halted them.

Gettis got up from his chair and stomped out of the house onto the low front porch and slumped in the wicker chair to wait for the three men to finish their chore. He had found no one in the house when he had entered. The Mexican housekeeper and her husband were gone, which meant Casey had probably told them to clear out, or to go visit their relatives or something. Both the Mexicans' wagon and Casey's buggy were gone.

And so was Casey, of course.

He had not the slightest doubt that this entire operation had been her idea from the start. She had used that poor son of a bitch Calder to get the gold into her buggy and had gone this far with him before . . . getting rid of him.

As he sat in the wicker chair and tried to sort out his feelings, one single, powerful emotion gradually assumed dominance, towering above everything else he felt. Betrayal. He had used the trust embodied in his sergeant's stripes to rob the army; and in a futile attempt to protect his scheme, he had killed the men he led in cold blood. Now he knew what it was to have the trust he vested in others so completely and utterly betrayed.

But he knew that Casey could not have carried this out entirely on her own. Strong-willed she was, and capable of harboring great fury; nevertheless, she did not have what it would take to crush Calder's skull like that. Gettis was certain of it. She must have had another accomplice. A man she knew, someone in Copper City. And if it was not Johnny Calder, then who in hell was it?

Custis Long came to mind almost immediately. He was gone too. And he had left the same day. Casey would have pulled out during the night more than likely so that no one would see her go, but that would not stop her from holding up to meet Long somewhere outside of town.

He got up out of the chair and began pacing, anxious to check this out. At last Slim and the others appeared from around the corner of the house, their expressions hangdog, their spirits chastened by the grisly task they had just performed. Without a word Gettis swung off the porch and headed across the yard to the street, the three hurrying after.

Behind the saloon Gettis found Casey's buggy tracks. Still ignoring his three bodyguards, he went down on one knee beside them, studying the impressions left by the four wheels. The tracks had been light enough when the wagon was driven up to the back door. But when it drove off—laden with the gold Casey and Calder had lugged out to it—the wheels' narrow rims dug deeply into the ground, and it was clear from the way the horses' hooves dug into the roadway to gain a more solid purchase that they were now laboring some. At least for a while, the gold-laden buggy would not be at all difficult to track.

Gettis stood up and addressed Slim. "Go get fresh horses and saddle them up."

As Slim hurried off to the livery, Gettis told the other two to get over to Stella's for provisions, enough for a

162

week at least, then load all their gear onto the horses. As they hurried off, Gettis strode from the alley and headed down the street to the hotel.

When he saw the intent, scowling face of Jim Gettis approaching, the desk clerk almost came to full attention. He was a young, narrow-shouldered fellow with thinning sandy hair and a barely visible mustache. He had always been more than willing to do Gettis's bidding, no questions asked.

"I need your help, Lars," Gettis said.

"Sure thing, Mr. Gettis."

"You sleep here in this hotel?"

"Yessir. I got a room in back. It ain't much, but—"

Gettis stopped him with an impatient wave of his hand. "Then maybe you see things around here—when you're off duty, I mean. Things you keep to yourself mostly. I ain't never heard of you tattlin' on guests."

"Oh, no, sir. I'd never do that."

"Then I can rely on your discretion."

"Absolutely, sir."

"The night before last, did you happen to notice if there was any unusual traffic in the back alley, and maybe on the back stairs? Say, on the town marshal's floor, for instance."

The desk clerk's Adam's apple danced as he swallowed and at once Gettis sensed that though his query had been a wild shot in the dark, it had been right on target. When he saw the cold sweat standing out on the desk clerk's forehead, Gettis leaned his face closer to him.

"I'm waitin', Lars."

"You . . . you ain't goin' to like this, Mr. Gettis."

163

Gettis smiled thinly. "You let me decide that. What did you see?"

Lars swallowed. "I saw Miss Casey."

Gettis smiled at Lars, almost gently. "Go on, Lars. I ain't surprised. You don't have to worry none. You just tell me what you saw—or heard."

Encouraged by Gettis's manner, Lars told of Casey pulling up in her buggy in the alley behind the hotel and of her use of the back stairs to gain the town marshal's second-floor room. He told Gettis just how long Casey had been up there, the significance of which was obviously not lost on him, and then recounted her driving off down the alley. Alone.

"Alone?"

Lars nodded. "Yes sir, Mr. Gettis."

Gettis slapped a gold twenty-dollar piece down on the counter in front of the clerk. "You keep this under your hat, Lars. Hear?"

"My lips are sealed, Mr. Gettis," the clerk said, sweeping up the gold coin.

"Just see they stay that way."

Gettis turned and strode purposefully from the hotel. He knew now all that he needed to know. Remembering that he had told Casey how long he might be gone, he realized she would not have expected him to have returned to Copper City as soon as he had. She—and Long—were counting on a lot more time than they really had.

As for where she was heading, he realized her buggy tracks would be clear only for a while, until the wind-driven sand sifted over them. But that didn't matter. All Casey had talked about for the past couple of months was San Francisco, and the closest stage linking up with the Southern Pacific was in Travis. Up until now, Gettis had been careful to keep himself well clear of the county seat, since Fort Crook was just outside it and the town would be crawling with men from the fort.

But it was still daylight, and if he could move fast enough, he could overtake them bastards long before they got near Travis.

Standing in her upstairs window, Carlotta watched the four horsemen riding out of town, heading northeast toward Travis. Jim Gettis was in the lead, his three henchmen eating his dust. There was a wild, sullen recklessness in the way Gettis led his men out of town, and Carlotta had a sense that he was acting out of a controlled fury so urgent that for the first time since she had known him, he had thrown his formidable caution to the wind. On this particular mission he would not be looking over his shoulder.

She heard the front door open, then close. She moved away from the window and peered over the bannister. MacDuff, weaving slightly, had just entered and was dropping his hat onto his peg on the rack under the stairs. She leaned her dust mop against the wall and waited for MacDuff to make his way up to her.

As he gained the second-floor landing, he saw her standing there and winked conspiratorially. "As you can see, Carlotta, I am in no condition to return to the newspaper this afternoon. If anyone comes looking for me, be so kind as to tell them you haven't seen me."

She nodded and without a word moved alongside him, taking his arm to help him down the hallway to his room. He leaned affectionately on her shoulder and let her open the door for him and help him inside. With great relief he sat wearily down on his bed, grinning foolishly up at Carlotta as he did so.

"Big doings, Carlotta," he told her.

"What's happening?" she asked. "I just saw Gettis and his men riding out of town."

"You mean you don't know? I thought the whole town knew by now."

"No, Mac. I do not know. I am with this mop all afternoon. It does not tell me much."

He nodded and took a deep breath. "Casey has run out on Gettis, and it seems she didn't leave empty-handed. She took half a month's of Gettis's proceeds with her." He shook his head in admiration. "That's a lot of gold, by my reckoning."

"She did that? By herself?"

"Ah, and there's the rub, Carlotta. At first it looked like Calder had gone off with her. But now it appears her help came from another source." He paused for dramatic effect.

"Yes?" she prompted impatiently. "Go on, Mac."

"It seems there's been some loose talk around town —about Casey and our new town marshal."

"Custis?"

He nodded, his eyes lit in admiration. "There's a man likes to play with fire. Casey's been seen visitin' him in his room—and he left for Travis the same day she left with the gold."

Carlotta took a deep breath. "And now Gettis is going after them."

"And he ain't lookin' back." MacDuff's tone became sober then. "Looks like Custis has bitten off more than he can chew this time. I wouldn't give a cent for Casey's chances either. Gettis can't afford to let them two get away with this. He'd be finished in this town if he did."

Carlotta smiled thinly, pleased in spite of her concern for Custis. It was good to know that Gettis had been stung in this fashion. He was a man now betrayed, a cuckold! His woman was in the hands of another—and had taken his gold, as well. All men knew of his shame, though none would speak to him openly of it. Only in their eyes would Gettis see their knowledge. How this must sting! She exulted.

MacDuff lay back onto his bed. Without being asked, Carlotta pulled off his shoes. He exhaled wearily, murmuring his thanks. She watched his eyes close, then turned and moved swiftly from the room, closing the door gently behind her. Then she raced lightly down the stairs to her own room.

Once inside it, she pulled a huge black trunk out from under her bed, unlatched it, and flung back the lid. With reverence then, she began to take from it her father's trousers, shirt, and vest, placing them neatly on top of her bed. This done, she reached under the bed for her father's black sombrero, his proudest possession. Placing it down on the bed beside the rest of her father's dress, Carlotta surveyed them with emotion, tears gleaming in the corners of her eyes.

She took a deep breath. This was not the time for tears, she chided herself. Now she must do what she had come to this town to accomplish. Gettis was unstrung. He would be careless—and only three of his bodyguards would be with him. And Custis Long would not be a man easy to kill. In all this confusion, this wild storm of hot lead, perhaps her chance would come. Then she would avenge her father's death.

167

But first, she must see to her horse and with great care clean her father's weapons.

She left the room and hurried out of the boarding-house, crossing to the livery where she quartered her horse. Dusk was already falling and she was anxious to be on her way before darkness overtook the land completely.

Chapter 12

Longarm had no intention of leaving Casey for the buzzards and took the time to locate a proper spot for the
burial site. He found what he wanted in the shade of the
bluff, the ground sloping gradually toward the east.
Using his rifle barrel to break through the ground and its
stock to shovel away the dirt, he buried Casey's body as
deep as he could, then covered the grave with a knee-
high pile of boulders to keep off the coyotes. Using a
strip of rawhide, he fashioned a cross out of two pieces
of greasewood, after which he took off his hat and
bowed his head over the cross for a moment or two,
wondering what in hell he could say for Casey that she
couldn't say for herself once she got to where she was
going. Then, looping her white lace collar over the
cross's vertical arm, he clapped on his hat, and went for
his horse.

Kincaid and the Mexicans had left the buggy and the two saddle horses Casey had brought with her. It was almost dark by this time and Longarm decided to make camp for the night and catch up with Kincaid and his party the next day. He selected a campsite high on the bluff, slept without a fire, and the next morning at the first crack of dawn, mounted up and spurred after Kincaid, the two saddle horses following, Indian fashion, on a lead behind him.

The tracks left by Kincaid's gold-laden mules were not difficult to follow and by mid-morning he found the campsite the three had used the night before and concluded they were not too far ahead of him. Mounting up, he drove his mount without mercy and broke out at last onto a ridge that gave him a clear, unobstructed view of the trail ahead.

Below him, almost swallowed up in the shimmering heat waves radiating from the baked ground, Kincaid's party inched across the desert, their gold-laden mules keeping them to a steady, measured pace. On the horizon before them sat the mountain range Longarm had glimpsed west of Copper City, a jagged rampart of snow-capped peaks that extended south clear into Mexico. Once Kincaid and his party reached that range it would be difficult, if not impossible, for Longarm to find, let alone overtake, them.

There was a sharp gap in the wall of peaks. Toward this pass Kincaid was heading. Longarm studied the terrain to the south. Paralleling the desert flat Kincaid was crossing, he noted, was a tortured land of rock, canyons, gulches, and steep, eroded benchlands. With a weary shrug Longarm decided that this badland would have to be his route if he were to head off Kincaid before he disappeared into the mountains.

Dismounting, he took his saddle off the livery horse he had ridden this far. It was close to exhaustion, but it had never faltered, giving him all the heart it had. He patted the animal affectionately on the flank, sending it off in search of water and fresh grass. He saddled up one of the saddle horses; then, still holding the lead to the other one, he slanted down the steep, gravelly slope and dropped into the badlands.

He found a trail following a broad streambed, which was as dry now as a bleached skull. For the most part the trail was smooth sand interspersed with stretches of gravel and caprock. Despite the heat, he kept his mount to a trot, lifting it to a lope whenever the trail ahead of him allowed. Halfway into the badlands he switched to the other horse, then changed back as soon as this mount began to labor. An hour or so before nightfall, he felt himself lifting into the foothills flanking the mountain range.

Picking out the crumbling wall of an old bluff, he headed for it. Once he had gained its crest, he found he had an excellent view of the desert he had just outflanked. A mile or so due north of him, Kincaid's party was just putting the desert behind them. He cut back off the ridge, released the other horse, and galloped toward the pass. Once insde it, he found a shaded pine grove, dismounted, took out a cheroot and smoked it down. Then he clambered up a rock face and peered back down the trail leading to the cut. Less than a hundred yards below him Kincaid and his party were coming to a halt on a pine-shaded flat. It was clear they had had it for that day. As Longarm watched, they set about making camp.

He pushed himself back off the rock and made his plans for that night.

171

Kincaid and his two Mexicans were cautious enough. They had built their camp fire against a rock face and had then carefully fashioned three dummy sleepers out of boulders and blankets, setting them close about the fire, after which they had retreated to safer spots, Kincaid choosing a site on the far slope. The only thing wrong with this elaborate precaution was the Longarm had been perched on a ledge above the camp fire watching the entire operation.

It was about two hours later now, and as the camp fire's dying flames played upon the dummy sleeping forms, they looked surprisingly lifelike. Had Longarm come upon their camp at nightfall, he might well have thought he was peering down at three quietly sleeping men.

It was time for the fireworks to begin. Leaning out over the ledge, Longarm dropped first one, then a second cartridge into the camp fire's glowing embers. He heard the first clicking against the ring of stones about the fire, but was not sure it had gone into it. Then he dropped three more, the embers leaping up slightly as each cartridge plunged into them. Satisfied, he brought up his Winchester and peered across at the slope facing him, his eyes on the spot where he had seen Kincaid bed down. He was not sure where the two Mexicans had curled up, but he was certain the upcoming firefight would cause them to reveal their positions.

Longarm had already jacked a fresh cartridge into the Winchester's firing chamber and he waited now with the safety off, his finger caressing the trigger. He took a deep breath, then exhaled slowly. Damn it. When were those cartridges going to start exploding?

Abruptly, the fireworks began.

In quick succession the camp fire erupted as two cartridges detonated, filling the air with the sound of the slugs ricocheting off the rock face. Another cartridge went off. And then another. And another. All this within the space of a few seconds.

Crouching low as the whining slugs seemed to fill the air, Longarm kept his eyes on the far slope. Suddenly a dark figure bolted from behind a clump of scrub pine, guns blazing as he fired at something he thought he saw to the right of the fire. Longarm tracked the dark form, aiming for a spot just above the gun flashes, and squeezed his trigger. Levering swiftly, he fired a second time.

Kincaid buckled and tumbled headfirst down the slope.

At once Longarm flattened himself on the ledge as a gun flash came from the pines to his right. A slug whanged off the ledge just below him. He swung his Winchester and poured a rapid fire into the spot the flash came from and heard a dim cry. Then he swung his rifle about, waiting for the second Mexican's gun flash. He knew the bastard was down there somewhere. Below him in the camp fire, what had to be the last cartridge detonated.

But instead of answering shots, Longarm heard running boots on the hard ground, the sound fading rapidly. A moment later came the clatter of hooves. The other Mexican was attempting flight.

Turning, Longarm raced back off the ledge, jumped to the ground and followed a narrow trail down the slope, heading for the flat. He broke out of a dark clump of pine in time to see a horse and rider emerge out of the gloom, pounding toward him. The Mexican had not yet

173

seen Longarm. It was too dark, the moon's light cut off by the towering peaks.

Longarm flung up his rifle and fired. He hit the horse in the chest, the sound of the slug's impact coming clearly to him. As the horse went down, the Mexican was flung forward over his head. He hit the ground less then ten yards in front of Longarm, leaped to his feet, and raced toward Longarm, a knife gleaming in his hand.

Longarm did not have enough time to reload and swing up his rifle. Ducking aside, he grabbed the barrel with both hands and swung the rifle like a baseball bat. He caught the onrushing Mexican in the gut, snapping him like a dry twig. He went down and stayed on the ground, writhing like a stomped worm, both arms wrapped about his gut.

Longarm levered swiftly and pointed the barrel down at the Mexican.

"Can you hear me?" Longarm asked.

"*Sí.*"

"I'm going to let you and your companion get out of this. He's been hit. Go back for him and take him out of here. You understand?"

Grimacing in pain, the Mexican managed to nod sullenly. "I un'erstand, *señor.*"

"All right, get up then, and lead the way back into your camp."

The Mexican pushed himself painfully to his feet and stumbled back to the campsite. Not long after, obviously unhappy to be leaving behind the gold, the two Mexicans rode off, the wounded one barely able to sit his horse, the one Longarm had struck with the rifle still grimacing in pain. Longarm figured their injuries would be enough of a constraint to keep them from doubling

174

back to take him, but of course he couldn't count on it.

He watched them go, then turned his attention to Kincaid's sprawled body. The man was on his side a few feet from the camp fire where he had come to rest. Poking through the fire to make sure there were no more cartridges, Longarm built it up again until it gave him enough light to examine Kincaid more closely.

The man's eyes flickered open as the heat from the leaping flames reached him. "It's you," he said, squinting at Longarm. "Damn you all to hell!"

"Shut up and let me look at your wounds."

Ripping apart Kincaid's shirt, Longarm saw that he had caught the man twice in the chest. The entry wounds were clean enough, but a man's chest was no place to carry hot lead. Longarm sat back on his haunches and studied Kincaid judiciously.

"You killed me, you son of a bitch," Kincaid said in a powerful, rasping whisper. A thin line of blood trickled from the corner of his mouth.

"You might make it to Travis," Longarm told him.

"Don't bother, you bastard."

Kincaid's eyes closed and he lost consciousness. Longarm stood up and studied the man solemnly. He had been serious. There *was* an outside chance Kincaid could live long enough to reach Travis. And since Longarm could not simply leave the man here to die—his silent vow to Casey had still been made good—he decided he had no choice but to make the attempt.

Leaving Kincaid, Longarm released the picketed mules, slapped a few hind ends, and watched them vanish down the slope. The sacks of gold had been piled neatly in a cleft alongside the rock that faced the camp fire. Filling it with pine needles, he piled rocks over them, then sand, after which he smoothed the ground with a branch.

Dispersing the bounders surrounding the camp fire and kicking the ashes away, he covered the site with sand and pine needles, again brushing the ground thoroughly with a branch. That done, he saddled up Kincaid's horse and draped the groaning, protesting deputy sheriff over it. Leading Kincaid's horse, he mounted up and rode back through the night and out of the pass.

A few hours before dawn, on the edge of the desert, he halted and made camp, a cliff wall at his back. Pulling Kincaid off his horse, Longarm examined the man and found he was still alive. Longarm shrugged. Hell, he might make it. More than once Longarm had seen men take bullets in the chest and survive.

He built a fire to warm Kincaid, then curled up beside it himself and dropped off almost at once into a profound sleep.

When he awoke, it was full daylight and Longarm was looking down a gun barrel. Somehow Kincaid had managed to crawl to Longarm's horse and pull the Winchester from its sling. Longarm flung aside his blanket and sat up.

"Put that away, Kincaid."

"I will. After I squeeze the trigger."

"You ain't thinking all that clear, Kincaid," Longarm drawled, "and I don't wonder at it, considering your condition. But the fact is, you ain't levered a fresh cartridge into the firing chamber yet, or I would've heard you—and the safety's still on."

Longarm's calm assertion froze Kincaid for just a moment, and with the speed of a striking snake, Longarm reached up and grabbed the rifle. As he yanked it from Kincaid's grasp, he ducked aside. Kincaid's finger managed to pull the trigger anyway, and the rifle detonated, sending a round whining off the rock wall behind them. Kincaid *had* levered a fresh cartridge into the firing chamber and *had* flicked off the safety.

Longarm was on his feet by this time, the rifle securely in his grasp.

"Nice try, Kincaid."

"Just leave me here," Kincaid said wearily, slumping back. "I don't want to go no farther."

Longarm knelt on one knee beside the wounded man. Kincaid's face was as white as bleached desert sand. The night's rest had done him little good, it seemed. His cheeks were sunken, his red-rimmed eyes peering at Longarm out of dark, hollow sockets in his skull.

He didn't look like he would last the day, let alone the journey to Travis. He blinked unhappily at Longarm. "Looks like the gold is all yours," he said.

"You could have had it, Kincaid. I don't want it. But I didn't like what you did to Casey."

"She dead?"

"That's right."

"She double-crossed me."

"That was her intent, I guess."

"She was Gettis's whore! How could you care about her?"

Longarm shrugged. "It's not easy to explain, Kincaid."

"Who the hell *are* you, mister? You been trouble since you first got off that stage. You ain't no drifter."

Longarm nodded. "That's right. I'm no drifter. I'm a deputy U.S. marshal."

"A federal marshal?"

Longarm nodded.

"Then you must've come after Gettis."

"That's right, Kincaid."

"Hell! You should've told me. I'd a helped you take him." He coughed in his excitement. "You should've let me!"

"You didn't give me the chance."

Longarm did not want to tell the dying man he would not have sided him under any circumstances. A corrupt lawman running a string of girls made a lousy partner in a gunfight.

"Get the bastard," Kincaid whispered hoarsely. He began to cough more violently, and now blood came with each paroxysm. It was not a pleasant sight to see a man cough his life out, and that was what he was doing. "Get Gettis for me, Long . . . !"

"No," Longarm said, standing up and taking a step back. "Not for you, Kincaid. But I'll get him."

"You sure of that, Long?"

The voice, heavy with malice, came from behind Longarm. Spinning about, Longarm saw Jim Gettis, flanked by his three bodyguards, stepping into view from behind the corner of the rock face. He was less than twenty feet away, his six-gun leveled at Longarm. His three bodyguards were each carrying rifles. Longarm was careful to keep the rifle in his own hand lowered.

"I saw where you buried Casey," Gettis said, walking toward Longarm. "Now, where's the gold?"

"I buried it."

Gettis walked past Longarm and stared down at the dying Kincaid. Kincaid was no longer coughing. Gettis kicked him in the side. It provoked no response. Gettis kicked him again, then leaned over Kincaid and spat in his face. The man was as dead as a rock.

"I thought it was you killed Calder," Gettis said, turning to Longarm.

"Johnny Calder's dead?"

"His skull smashed in."

"It wasn't me."

"Then it was Kincaid did it. And he helped Casey take the gold."

Longarm nodded. "I knew nothing about Kincaid or the gold—not until Casey told me about it before she died."

Gettis regarded Longarm carefully. "No, it's not gold you're after. I just heard you. It's my scalp you want."

"Something like that."

"Forget me, Long. Take the gold. Go ahead. It's yours. Ride out with it. Leave me be. Tell your superiors that Jim Gettis is not Sergeant Cable, that you couldn't find him. Do that and I'll let you live."

"I wish I could say I was tempted, Gettis."

"Then, damn you! You'll die here!"

"There'll be others to come after you, Gettis. Killing a U.S. deputy marshal will only bring the sky down on you."

"What choice do I have?"

"Give me that revolver and ride to Fort Crook as my prisoner. Take your chances with the law."

"You must think I'm crazy. You know what an army court-martial will do to me."

"Then you'll just have to kill me."

Gettis's face went hard with resolve. But before he could lift his revolver, Longarm flung the rifle he had been holding at the man, knocking him back. At the same time he threw himself sideways to the ground, rolled over, and kept rolling as Gettis's bodyguards snapped hasty shots at him. Drawing his double-action

.44 as he rolled, he came up firing at the three men, one round slamming into Mac high enough on his shoulder to send him tumbling backward into a gully. Shorty caught a slug in his gut and doubled over.

Slim held his ground and fired coolly at Longarm, his slug hitting the revolver and knocking it from Longarm's grasp. Longarm lay perfectly still, his hand resting on the double-barreled derringer in his vest pocket, and watched as Gettis and Slim strode closer, both men's expressions hard with resolve.

"You bastard," said Slim, staring down at Longarm. "You caught Shorty bad. He's gut-shot." He started to lever a fresh cartridge into his Winchester's firing chamber.

"No," said Gettis, his voice harsh. He pushed Slim to one side and stepped closer to Longarm. "Let me finish the son of a bitch."

Palming the derringer, Longarm flung it up and fired at Gettis, the .44 slug entering under his chin and ranging up into his skull, causing it to explode outward. Longarm turned his derringer on Slim then, discharging his remaining round; but Slim was quick and ducked low and to the side, the slug whining off a tree behind him.

Straightening up, Slim kicked the empty derringer out of Longarm's hand, then cranked the lever of his Winchester and fitted the stock into his hip, aiming point-blank down at Longarm.

"Don't you want to know where the gold is?" Longarm asked him.

Slowly, the man lowered the barrel. "Sure. Where is it?"

"I'll take you to it."

"The hell you will. We saw the tracks them Mexican's left. They took it from you two."

"That's not the truth."

"I don't believe you, you bastard." Resolve again hardened his features and he lifted his rifle again.

From high above came the sharp, echoing crack of a rifle.

Slim looked as if he were going to cry, then all expression left his face and he fell forward, landing face-down. Longarm saw the hole in his back and leaped to his feet, snatching up Slim's rifle as he scanned the rock face leaning over him.

The shot had come from up there, he was certain. But whether it had been meant for him or for Slim he was not all that sure. Abruptly, the third bodyguard Longarm had sent backward into the gully clambered into view, his six-gun out and blazing.

In his condition, his shots were not all that accurate, his wild fire chewing up the ground in front of Longarm, who went down on one knee, aimed carefully, and returned Mac's fire. The man flipped backward and disappeared a second time into the gully. Longarm stood up then and looked warily around him, wondering who in hell had shot down Slim.

He heard hooves. Swinging around in the direction from which the sound came, he saw a rider coming into view from around the rock face. He must have come from the rocks above.

He was a Mexican riding a powerful blue and was dressed in the manner of the Spanish caballeros of old, in black leather trousers, silken shirt, and black leather vest. On his head sat a fine, brilliantly decorated sombrero, the wide brim keeping his face in shadow, so that

181

all Longarm could make out as he rode closer was his smooth, determined jawline.

This was the one whose bullet had brought down Slim, saving Longarm's life in the bargain. Longarm started eagerly forward to greet his benefactor, then pulled up, astonished. The Mexican had swept off his sombrero—and Longarm found himself staring up at Carlotta, a gleaming, freshly cleaned Sharps resting across her pommel.

"How you like that shot?" she asked, pulling her mount to a halt before him.

"That was you?"

"Yes," she said proudly. "It was my father who show me how to use this rifle."

She leaned forward and dropped the rifle in its sling, then slipped off the blue and strode toward him. Longarm hesitated only an instant, then opened his arms to her.

Longarm sat up in the bed and saw Carlotta standing naked in the window, her lush figure outlined clearly in the moonlight. It was the sound she made slipping out of bed that had awakened him. He looked at her for a while, then flipped aside his covers and came up behind her, gently fitting his nakedness against her. She laughed softly and leaned back into him.

"What is it?" he asked. "What awakened you?"

"I was thinking of how long I wait to kill Jim Gettis —and then I am not the one who do it."

"You should be relieved. Taking on Gettis was my job. Not yours."

"All the same, I feel cheated."

"He's dead. His men are scattered to the four winds. His reign is over. The King is dead."

"Yes, I know." She turned to face him, put her arms around his neck and pressed herself into him. "Long Live the King."

"But only for a while," he reminded her. "You read the telegram. I have three weeks to settle this place down before the sheriff in Travis appoints another deputy sheriff."

"Yes. Three weeks. It will go fast for you, Custis. I promise you."

He kissed her and led her back to the bed. "Have you contacted your people?" he asked.

She nodded. "Yes," she said. "Already they are taking back the land Gettis take from them."

"Good."

He lay back on the bed and pulled her onto him. She moved just enough to make it possible for him to enter her. She smiled down, her eyes lidded, her mouth parted slightly so that he could see the gleaming whiteness of her teeth.

"Tomorrow you take me to the gold?" she hissed softly.

"Yes."

"Are you sure you can find it?"

"Don't worry."

"My people will use it to rebuild the valley. There is much one can do with all that gold. It will make them able to fight off the gringos who come to take the land again."

"That's right. You can hire gringo lawyers."

"You are so kind." She leaned back onto him and began to move slowly. He enjoyed it very much. "Are you sure no one will know where this gold come from?

"As long as you don't tell them."

183

"Is it legal, what you do? Give it to me and my people?"

"I don't know. And I won't try to find out. Just make good use of it."

"Oh, yes," she cried, sucking in her breath. "We will do that."

She was driving him mad. "Let's not talk any more about it," he gasped.

But she was way ahead of him, her head flung back, her long raven tresses enveloping him in a fragrant tent. He had hoped they could get an early start the next morning, but realized now that this would be out of the question.

So they'd get a late start.

LONGARM

Explore the exciting Old West with
one of the men who made it wild!